Three-Ring Terror

Joe reached out to grab Costello as the criminal stepped off the platform and was swept away on the trapeze. Joe had only one choice—take the other trapeze swing and go! He swung off the platform, flying through the air in a long, breathtaking arch.

But Costello used that time to let himself land back on the platform from which he'd jumped in the first place. Somehow, Joe had to get back there, too. There was just one problem. He was going to have to turn around.

Joe held his breath and said to himself, "Here goes nothing." With that, he let go of the swing with one hand. Below, the crowd drew in a long breath. For a split second Joe was airborne. Then he twisted his body around and caught the swing with the other hand. He did it!

Joe swung back to the platform, where Costello was waiting for him. As soon as Joe felt himself land squarely on the platform, he also felt Costello's fist meet his jaw.

The Hardy Boys Mystery Stories

Available from MINSTREL Books

111

The
HARDY BOYS®

THREE-RING TERROR

FRANKLIN W. DIXON

A MINSTREL® BOOK

PUBLISHED BY POCKET BOOKS

New York   London   Toronto   Sydney   Tokyo   Singapore

A MINSTREL PAPERBACK *ORIGINAL*

A Minstrel Book published by
POCKET BOOKS, a division of Simon & Schuster Inc.
1230 Avenue of the Americas, New York, NY 10020

Copyright © 1991 by Simon & Schuster Inc.
Cover illustration copyright © 1991 by Paul Bachem
Produced by Mega-Books of New York, Inc.

ISBN: 0-671-73057-6

First Minstrel Books printing December 1991

10 9 8 7 6 5 4 3 2 1

Printed in the U.S.A.

Contents

THREE-RING
TERROR

1 Juggling a Mystery

"Chet, you're really serious about learning to become a clown, aren't you?" Frank Hardy said to his friend.

"Definitely!" Chet Morton exclaimed. He readjusted the fuzzy orange wig on his head. A huge grin spread across his wide, painted red clown mouth. "Circus University—better known as Circus U.—is the biggest thing to hit Bayport in years."

"That costume's pretty big, too," Frank's younger brother, Joe, said with a smile. Joe shook his head as he stared at the polka-dotted clown costume Chet wore. The costume had huge ballooning arms and legs, and a big, white pleated collar. Chet's a big guy to begin with, Joe re-

1

flected, and that costume makes him look even bigger.

"Give Chet a break, Joe," Frank said. "Circus U. has trained some of the most famous clowns in the country."

Frank, who was six-foot-one and eighteen years old, ran his hands through his dark brown hair and looked around the backstage area of the Bayport Arena. Circus performers passed by, carrying props and leading trained animals. Every so often, applause could be heard from the arena, where the opening-night performance of the Montero Brothers Circus was in progress.

A blond woman dressed in a tuxedo led a striped tiger on a leash to the table where Chet and another young man were serving soft drinks and popcorn to circus performers, Circus U. students, and a group of guests who had been invited to mingle with the performers backstage.

"Be careful," Joe said jokingly, pulling Frank out of the tiger's way. "We wouldn't want anything to happen to Bayport's finest detective."

Frank smiled as the tiger blinked at him sleepily. "This guy doesn't look too dangerous," he said. The tiger yawned and pawed the ground.

"Don't be so sure," the blond woman warned, leading the tiger away. "Let's go, Grumpy. We're on next."

"Grumpy! That's a great name," Joe said, his blue eyes lighting up with amusement. Joe had blond hair and, at seventeen, was almost as tall as his brother.

"This is really exciting, isn't it?" Chet asked his friends. He gestured to the crowd of performers milling around them.

"It sure is," Frank agreed. The backstage area was beginning to fill up with performers waiting to go out to the arena. There were acrobats and clowns and a man dressed like Uncle Sam walking on stilts. Frank saw a clown-faced juggler wearing a blue wig, an orange T-shirt, and baggy striped pants with suspenders toss five gem-studded metal balls high in the air, catch each ball, then grin and bow as a small group of guests applauded.

Frank peered through a crack in the red curtain to his right.

"What's happening out there?" Chet asked, standing on tiptoe to look over Frank's shoulder.

"Grumpy is doing his act," Frank reported. He watched as the blond woman guided her trained tiger through a hoop.

"Let me see," Joe said, pushing past Frank to look through the curtain. "He's jumping through two hoops. Incredible!"

Frank stepped out of his younger brother's way. He liked the circus, but it wasn't nearly as exciting as investigating a case, which was what he really enjoyed. He and Joe were well known around Bayport, and beyond, as detectives. Being without a mystery to solve made Frank restless.

"The Montero Brothers Circus has to be the best there is," Chet shouted over the noise of the applauding crowd in the arena.

Joe turned and asked his friend, "What makes this circus so special?"

Chet readjusted his wig. "Boy, does this thing itch," he said with a grimace. He poured a soft drink for another clown, then turned back to Frank and Joe. "I did a lot of research on the Montero Brothers Circus before I applied for this clown internship," he said. "The circus was started by two trapeze artists, Carlos and Armando Montero, back in the nineteen-fifties. It's one of the most famous circuses in the country."

"Why would you need a clown internship?" Joe asked. "You were already voted class clown last year."

"Ha, ha," Chet said. "Laugh now, but once I'm done taking these classes at Circus U., there's a chance I might someday go to the university full time to become a real clown."

"A *real* clown?" Frank asked, pointing at Chet's costume. "What are you now? A fake clown?"

"No. I mean yes. Come on, guys, give me a break."

Frank laughed, and Joe said, "Okay, Chet, we'll lay off. Tell us about Circus U."

"Circus University trains the top circus performers," Chet explained. "Most of the performers you're seeing today got their start at Circus U."

"People actually study to do this?" Frank asked, pointing to a nearby juggler. "Can't you learn all these tricks on your own?"

"The tricks look easier than they really are," Chet said. "You have to learn how to do these tricks correctly and safely. Circus U. teaches you everything there is to know—juggling, clowning, trapeze, high wire, the works. And it brings in outside performers to teach the students, people who are famous for their work in circuses all across the country."

"Pretty impressive," Joe said. "What's the connection between Circus U. and the circus that's performing today?" he asked.

"Circus U. is based in Florida, but it travels around the country for several months each year offering classes to high school students who might be interested in becoming circus performers some day," Chet explained. "Circus U. travels with the Montero Brothers Circus so that full-time students and part-timers like me can see what it's like to work with a real circus."

"When the Montero Brothers Circus leaves Bayport, will Circus U. go with it?" Frank asked.

Chet nodded his head yes and his orange wig

nearly fell off. He reached up to straighten it. "But some of the faculty will head back to Florida to get ready for spring semester."

Frank peered through the red curtains again. The performance in the arena was coming to an end. The crowd was giving the circus performers a standing ovation, and the applause and cheers were getting louder. Off to Frank's right, a television camera was catching the last bows of the circus performers.

"You guys should come back tomorrow and watch the whole show from out front," Chet shouted over the noise of the crowd.

"Maybe we will," Joe said. "I never got to see the clown acts tonight."

"Who are all these guests backstage?" Frank asked Chet as they moved back toward the refreshment table. "Do they work for the circus or are they students at Circus U.?"

"Both," Chet said. "The circus is hosting this opening-night reception for their performers and Circus U. employees and students. There are also some Circus U. VIPs here and guests from the community."

"So when do you start school?" Joe asked. "You must be pretty excited."

"You bet," Chet agreed. "I start tomorrow. A whole week of training with the best clown teachers in the business. I can't wait."

"I can't believe you're spending the whole week of winter vacation learning to become a clown," Joe said, shaking his head.

"Hey, isn't that what vacation's for—clowning around?" Chet asked, grinning.

Joe laughed, "I guess you're right."

Chet reached down under the table. "Look what the university gave me." He held up a red, white, and blue tote bag. The words "Circus University" were printed on the side of the bag in bright orange lettering. "It's for my clown gear," he explained. "And I get to keep the clown suit after my classes are over."

"A week of Chet acting like a clown," Frank said to Joe. "What are we in for?"

Joe nodded. "I know what you mean," he said. "Let's just hope he stays far away from us when he's learning the seltzer trick."

The backstage area was beginning to fill up with performers and guests. "I'd better get back to work," Chet said, stowing his tote bag back under the table. "I would hate to have Bo Costello see me goofing off when I'm supposed to be handing out refreshments."

"Who's Bo Costello?" Joe wanted to know.

"My boss," Chet explained. He pulled a bag of ice from under the table and started filling up a pitcher with fresh punch.

"Your boss is named Bo Costello?" Frank said.

"Well, he's not my boss, exactly," Chet said. "Can I get you guys some punch?" he asked. "A soda? Glass of water?"

"I'll take a soda," Joe said. "So, who *is* Bo Costello?"

"He's only the director of admissions at Circus U.," Chet replied.

"Sorry, Chet, but Joe and I aren't exactly up on who's who at Circus U.," Frank said with a grin.

"Costello's one of the most important people at Circus U. When I stopped by his office yesterday to get the class schedule and a catalog, he mentioned that he needed people to work the refreshment table tonight. When he said I'd get to wear my clown gear, I volunteered."

"Look out," Frank warned. The clown-faced juggler he'd seen earlier was about to step right into Joe. Frank pulled his brother from the path of the juggler.

"Sorry," the juggler said, dropping several of his gem-studded balls. Each ball had different colored gems, and they sparkled brightly under the lights. The juggler's striped green pants were covered with flecks of rhinestones that matched the studs on the ball.

"I guess I wasn't watching where I was going," the juggler said apologetically as he leaned over to pick up the balls.

"That's okay," Frank said. "We were in your way." He leaned down to pick up a ball that had

8

fallen at his feet, but the juggler grabbed the ball off the floor before Frank could touch it. Shoving the balls into the pockets of his baggy green pants, the juggler then quickly rounded the table to find another ball that had rolled underneath it.

"So what kind of classes are you taking?" Joe turned to ask Chet.

"Let's see. Juggling, of course. And some magic tricks. There's a makeup class, too."

While Chet went on, Frank stepped around to the side of the table. He spotted the juggler kneeling on the ground behind the table. "It's right there," Frank told him, pointing to the ball that was lying next to Chet's Circus U. bag.

But the juggler didn't hear him, and Frank quickly figured out why. He was too busy rifling through Chet's bag!

2 A Circus Code

"Hey! Get your hands out of there!" Frank yelled. "That's my friend's bag."

"What's going on?" Joe said as soon as he heard Frank's shout.

The juggler looked up and saw Frank standing over him. He leaped up from his crouch beside the table and pushed Frank aside.

Frank fell onto the refreshment table, and it collapsed under him with a crash. The crowd that had gathered jumped out of the way. Then Frank felt cold drinks and popcorn spilling on top of him.

"Frank!" Chet cried. "What—"

Frank pulled himself off the table. "Later,

Chet!" he exclaimed. "Come on, Joe. We've got to stop that juggler."

The Hardys pushed their way through a crowd of circus performers who were coming backstage through the red velvet curtain. Frank spotted the juggler's blue wig weaving through the crowd. When the juggler reached the curtain that led to the arena, he paused to let a group of men and women in matching spangled leotards and tights go around him.

"There he is," Frank said, pointing him out to Joe.

"Let's get him!" Joe cried.

Just then, the juggler disappeared through the curtain. The Hardys pushed their way through the crowd and followed the juggler into the arena. Their progress was slowed by the parade of performers that was continuing to move toward the backstage area.

"We're going to lose him in this crowd," Joe said.

"Not if I can help it," Frank muttered between his teeth.

Frank tried to keep his eye on the tall, broad-shouldered figure of the juggler, but a man in a tuxedo and a woman dressed in an acrobat's costume cut in front of them. By the time Frank had pushed past them, the juggler was gone.

"Rats," Frank said, moving away from the

11

crowd and stopping short in the middle of the arena. "Where'd he go?"

Joe looked around the huge space. Three large circus rings had been set up in the arena with trapezes, a high wire, and brightly painted platforms for animal acts. Seats for the audience stretched upward and in a semicircle around the arena. "He could have gone anywhere," Joe said. "There are exits at the end of every aisle of seats, plus those two fire exits at each side of the arena."

Frank nodded. The juggler might have sneaked out through any one of the clearly marked exits.

"I'll look for him outside," Frank said, pointing to the closest red exit sign. "You look around the backstage area. Check out dressing rooms and offices."

"Right," Joe said with a nod. "Meet you at Chet's table in fifteen minutes." He turned and hurried back toward the red velvet curtain.

Frank quickly headed to his left, in the direction of the exit sign. As soon as he pushed the door open, a blast of cold, damp air greeted him. Frank shivered in his wet shirt, which had been drenched with punch. The December night was brisk, and it felt as if it might snow. Frank circled the arena parking lot, passing between parked cars and looking underneath them. Streetlights at corners of the lot gave off some light, but not enough for Frank to spy the juggler. Finally, he checked his watch and saw that his fifteen minutes were up. Time to meet Joe, he thought with frustration, and he didn't have anything solid to report. The juggler had escaped.

Frank hurried back into the building. He could at least find out what, if anything, was missing from Chet's bag. Then they could report the theft to the Circus U. authorities. If the juggler was with the circus, or a student at Circus U., they'd find him soon enough.

His brother was waiting for him on the other side of the curtain.

"No luck?" Joe asked when he saw the look of disappointment on Frank's face.

Frank shook his head. "How about you?" he asked.

"I checked a couple of storage rooms and the men's locker room. Nothing. The guy disappeared. Let's find out what he took," he suggested, leading the way back to the refreshment table.

Chet had righted the table, mopped up the mess, and gone back to pouring punch and sodas for the thirsty crowd. Every once in a while he stopped to readjust his wig. "Hey, what happened?" Chet called out when he spotted Frank and Joe. "Did you find that guy?"

"No luck," Frank answered, leaning down to pick up Chet's Circus U. tote bag. "But I saw him with his hands in your bag."

"You're kidding," Chet said, reaching for the bag. "I hope none of my Circus U. stuff is gone."

"What's this?" Frank asked as he felt a round metallic object underneath a pair of Chet's jeans. He pulled the object out of the bag. It was a green, studded ball.

"That's just like the ball the juggler lost under the table," Joe said.

"Right," Frank said, holding up the ball. It was the size of a softball but much heavier. Dotted all along the outside were penny-size gems that looked like rhinestones. With his other hand, Frank passed the tote bag over to Chet. "Check to see if there's anything missing," he told his friend.

Chet nodded and started going through his bag. Joe reached for the ball and gave Frank a quizzical look. "The question is, what's it doing in Chet's bag?" he asked his brother.

Frank shrugged. "You got me. But the juggler must have had some reason for stashing this ball in Chet's bag." He took the ball back from Joe and continued to examine it.

Chet held up his tote bag. "Everything's here, including my wallet," he told Frank and Joe. "That's weird, isn't it?"

Frank ran his hands over the gem-studded ball. "It sure is. But it's an important clue, too," he said.

"Why?" Chet wanted to know.

14

"It means we're not dealing with some common crook," Joe told him.

"Well, if he's not a common crook, then who is he?" Chet asked.

"That's what we have to find out," Frank said. He thought for a moment. "Let's ask around. See if anyone knows who the juggler is."

"Sorry I'm late," a man's voice called out. Frank turned around and saw a clown, dressed like Chet in a blue and white polka-dotted suit and an orange wig, standing by the table. He was about the same height as Chet and looked to be in his early twenties. "The name's Carl Nash," the man told Chet in a cheerful southern drawl. "I'm here to relieve you all."

"I'm Chet Morton," Chet said. He looked at his watch. "Bo told me someone would show up to take over right about now."

Nash grinned as he looked around the backstage area. "It's pretty busy, isn't it? I'd better get started pouring punch for these thirsty people," he said. With that, Nash edged his way past Frank and stationed himself behind the table. He took a quick look at the ball in Frank's hand, smiled, and drawled slowly, "Nifty prop. Are you all Circus U. students from Bayport, too?"

Instead of answering Carl Nash's question, Frank said, "One of the jugglers must have lost a ball. Got any idea who it could have been?"

"Can't say I do," Nash replied, putting some

15

ice in a cup and pouring a drink for a little boy who stood by the table.

"Where are you from?" Joe asked Nash.

Nash's bright blue eyes lit up behind his white clown makeup. "Funny you should ask. Not from around here, that's for darn sure."

"I didn't think so, from your accent, that is," Frank offered.

"You got it," Nash said, raising his bushy orange eyebrows. "I'm a good ol' boy from deep in the heart of Texas."

"Are you a student at Circus U.?" Chet asked eagerly.

"That's right." Nash's clown mouth spread into a wide red smile. "I graduate this year. Trapeze is my specialty."

"Wow," Chet said, impressed. "I guess you're not afraid of heights then."

Joe laughed. "He'd better not be."

"I used to be," Nash said with a chuckle. "But I got over it pretty fast."

"I'll bet," Frank said. He kept passing the ball back and forth between his hands. "Are you ready to go, Chet?"

"If Carl thinks he can handle the crowd on his own," Chet said, turning to the trapeze student.

"No problem," Nash said. "It's thinning out, anyway. There are just a few circus folks and some VIPs left, from what I can tell," he added, scanning the crowd. "Go on home."

"Thanks," Chet told him, pulling off his wig and putting it in his tote bag. "I'm just glad to be able to take this thing off," he said with a grin.

"I know what you mean," Nash said, scratching at his wig. "It sure does itch. Oh," he went on, turning to Frank and Joe. "I almost forgot. Why don't you two guys come with your friend to class tomorrow? Circus U. is having an open house for students and friends. You'll also get to watch the circus performers in rehearsal. It should be fun."

Chet's eyes lit up. "That's a great idea." He turned to the Hardys. "I can give you guys a behind-the-scenes tour of the circus."

Frank looked at Joe. "What do you think?" he asked.

"Why not," Joe answered. "We are on vacation after all."

"Thanks for the invitation," Frank said to Carl Nash. "We'll see you tomorrow then."

"Great," Nash said. He went back to working the refreshment stand.

"He seems like a nice guy," Chet commented as he and Joe followed Frank away from the refreshment table.

"Maybe he can show you some tricks on the trapeze," Joe said, grinning.

Chet shook his head emphatically. "Not me. No way. This clown stays on the ground."

17

Frank led them to a less crowded part of the backstage area. He stopped at the edge of a room filled with circus props.

"Why are we stopping?" asked his brother.

"We need to plan our strategy," Frank replied. "How we're going to find out who that juggler was, why he left this"—Frank held up the gem-studded ball—"in Chet's bag, and what it all means."

Chet bit his lip thoughtfully, smearing his red makeup. "Why don't we just turn the ball in to the circus officials and let them take care of finding out the answers to all those questions."

"Come on, Chet," Joe said. "Where's your sense of adventure?"

"You two are the detectives," Chet replied. "I'm here to learn how to be a clown, not to solve mysteries."

"But Frank and I will need your help," Joe pointed out. "You're in a perfect position to supply us with info on the people here."

"Look, you guys," Chet went on, shaking his head in exasperation. "Don't mess things up for me, okay? If you start snooping around here, the circus people might not like it, and then I could be in trouble."

"Wait a minute," Frank said. "Since when have we put solving a case above our friendship?"

Chet frowned slightly. "Never, I guess. But don't do it now, either, okay?"

18

"Deal," Frank said, reaching out to shake Chet's hand. The polka-dotted sleeve of Chet's costume flapped wildly as Frank pumped Chet's hand. "So tell us," Frank continued, "who should we talk to tomorrow to find out who that juggler is?"

Chet shook his head and shrugged. "You got me. So far, I've only met Bo Costello. You could ask him, I guess."

"Sounds good to me. Have you got any ideas, Joe?" Frank asked his brother.

"Let's take another look at the ball," Joe suggested. "Maybe there's something about it we missed the first time we looked at it."

"True," Frank said, squinting at the ball. "This may be an ordinary prop, but who knows?"

He held the ball up to the light. The white gems looked like rhinestones or glass, but he took out his pocketknife and scraped at each one of them just to be sure. The gems flaked away under the pressure of the knife. "That tells us one thing, at least."

"What's that?" Chet asked.

"The gems aren't real," Joe explained to Chet. "Otherwise, the knife wouldn't have scratched them."

Frank looked at the ball carefully again. This time, he saw a thin seam running around the middle of the ball. "I think I've found something," he told Joe, pointing out the seam.

19

"Try twisting the ball to see if it opens," Joe suggested.

Frank turned the ball over in his hands. Sure enough, Joe was right. The two halves turned and the ball popped open. A small folded-up piece of paper fell out and fluttered to the ground.

Joe picked up the paper and unfolded it. "Weird," he said, handing the paper to his brother. "Definitely weird."

Frank looked at the paper. On it were three pairs of letters with numbers written on them.

"Are you thinking what I'm thinking?" Joe asked his brother.

Frank nodded. "It looks like we've just found some kind of coded message!"

3 The Human Cannonball

"Well, what do you know," Joe said, looking at the slip of paper. "I get the feeling our juggler friend left us with more of a mystery than we thought."

"I wonder what this code means," Chet said, taking the paper from Joe and reading the figures 1220, 103, and 214. "That's a strange set of numbers," he remarked.

"And look at the letters next to them," Frank said, pointing. "CN, JL, GU. I don't see any patterns, do you?"

Joe thought for a moment, quickly running down a sequence of simple codes he'd learned over the years. "Nope," he said finally. "Frank, if this really is a coded message, that juggler was passing information, whether he knew it or not."

"But why was he passing information to me?" Chet asked.

Joe shook his head. "Who knows? But I think we had better try to find out." He looked around the backstage area. The place was clearing out. Most of the guests had gone, and only a few circus performers remained. "I doubt we'll learn anything here tonight, though," Joe said.

"You're right," Frank agreed. "Let's go home and see if we can crack this code."

"Hey, guys," Chet protested, pointing to the two halves of the gem-studded ball in Frank's hand. "We can't leave here with that. It belongs to the circus, or Circus U., depending on who that juggler was. We have to return it."

Joe reached out for the ball, which Frank had put back together. "We will," he said firmly. "As soon as we find out just who this mystery juggler is and what he's doing passing coded information."

The next morning, Joe woke up bright and early. He got out of bed, showered, and went down to the kitchen, taking the coded message with him.

He read the numbers and letters on the slip of paper: CN—1220, JL—103, GU—214. "There's got to be some way to crack this code," he muttered to himself as he sat at the table and poured himself a bowl of cereal.

Joe was still at it when Frank came down to breakfast half an hour later. "Any luck?" his brother asked, opening the refrigerator and taking out a pitcher of juice.

"Nope," Joe said, shaking his head and staring once more at the arrangement of letters and numbers.

"Where is everyone?" Frank asked, sitting down next to his brother.

"Dad left a note saying he had to go out of town to the police headquarters in Philadelphia to run a check on someone. A new case, I guess."

Frank nodded. The brothers' father, Fenton Hardy, was a private investigator, and his hours often started early and ended late. "What about Mom and Aunt Gertrude?" he asked.

"They left a note saying they'd be gone all day," Joe said, looking up for a second from the coded message. "They're visiting friends in New York."

"We'd better hurry if we're going to pick up Chet," Frank said. He checked his watch. "You shouldn't have let me sleep this late."

Joe stood up, stuffed the paper in the pocket of his jeans, and headed for the kitchen door. "I was busy trying to crack this code and I lost track of time," he said, grabbing his jacket from the coatrack by the door.

After the Hardys had picked up Chet, Frank drove the brothers' black police van toward the Bayport Arena. On the way, the three of them talked about the mystery juggler.

"Do you think he was a spy, passing secret information?" Chet asked. "That would be too much, wouldn't it?"

Joe laughed and twisted around in the front seat to look at Chet. His friend wasn't wearing his clown costume but had his Circus U. tote bag with him. "We shouldn't jump to any conclusions," Joe said. "At least not until we ask around and find out just who this guy is."

Frank steered the van into the arena parking lot. "We still need to find out what the message means," he said. "And why he dropped the ball in your bag."

"The ball!" Joe exclaimed, slapping his forehead with his palm. "We left it at home."

Frank shot his brother a look as he switched off the ignition. "You mean, *you* left it at home."

"You were the one who rushed me out of the house," Joe protested. "If you hadn't overslept, this wouldn't have happened."

"Hey, guys," Chet said, crawling over the seat to follow Joe out the passenger side of the van. "It's no big deal. You can go home and get it after Dean Turner's speech."

"Who's Dean Turner?" Frank asked.

"He's the dean of Circus U.," Chet answered.

"He's giving a speech this morning about Circus U. for students and guests. And then he's going to perform a trick he used to be famous for."

"Oh, great," Joe said absently. He was still mad at himself for leaving the juggler's ball in his room. He could see it now, sitting on top of his desk where he'd left it the night before.

"Dean Turner's going to be shot out of a cannon," Chet said. "Isn't that neat?"

"Definitely," Frank said. He looked at his brother, who was staring off into space, a glum expression on his face. "Forget about the ball, Joe. We don't really need it to find out who the mystery juggler is."

"I guess you're right," Joe agreed reluctantly. "All we really have to do is describe the ball and see if anyone with the Montero Brothers Circus or Circus U. knows a guy who wears green rhinestone-covered pants and a blue wig and juggles gem-studded balls."

"Exactly," Frank said. "It just means a little more legwork."

"Let's move it," Chet urged, looking at his watch. "We've only got fifteen minutes before Dean Turner's speech."

The Hardys and Chet headed across the parking lot. Chet led them around to the back of the Bayport Arena. It was cold out, but the sun shone brightly, reflecting off the stark white walls of the huge, round, domed building.

"Where are we going?" Joe asked as Chet opened a door marked Private.

"This is the entrance to the arena's offices and multipurpose rooms," Chet explained as they stepped into the building. "I want to give you a quick tour of our classrooms."

Chet turned left and led the Hardys down a hallway that curved past a bank of elevators.

"This is where we learn makeup," Chet said, pointing to a room on their left. He opened the door to the next room. "And here's the prop classroom."

Joe saw the room was full of wood, paint, and worktables. There was even a huge table saw and drill. The room looked a lot like his shop class in school. "You have to make your own props?" he asked.

Chet nodded. "Every clown learns how to make his or her own props. That's part of building a clown character."

Frank let out a whistle. "Boy, you're serious about this clowning thing, aren't you?"

Chet grinned. "As serious as any clown can be."

They continued down the hall. When they reached the elevators, Chet said, "Down the rest of the hallway are the offices for arena employees and the offices Circus U. people are using. The circus animals are also kept down here. The elevators lead to the arena and locker rooms."

"I searched around the locker rooms and down here when I was looking for the juggler last night," Joe said.

The Hardys and Chet rode one of the passenger elevators up to the main floor. They walked down a short hallway toward double glass doors that said Entrance to Arena.

When they stepped through the doors, they found themselves at the top of the last aisle of seats. Way below them were the three circus rings. A cannon was placed in the middle of the center ring, and there was a podium next to it. The seats were beginning to fill up with families and students. Some of the students were dressed in leotards and sweatshirts and had Circus U. tote bags with them.

"Let's get a good seat," Chet urged. "I want to be up close."

"Not too close," Frank said with a grin. "We don't want Dean Turner to come flying right at us."

The three friends took seats in the third row of the center section. Joe noticed that there was a safety net strung up in front of the seats on his right, and that the cannon was pointed at the net. He nudged Frank and pointed to the net. "Just in case you were really worried that we'd be hit by the human cannonball," he said, smiling.

Soon the bleachers around them were full of students and parents with young children.

"How many students are there at Circus U.?" Joe asked Chet.

Chet scanned the crowd. "There are ten from Bayport High. I'm not sure how many full-timers are interning with the Montero Brothers Circus."

Just then a short, thin man with dark hair and glasses stepped up to the podium. He was wearing a tweed coat and brown slacks. Joe thought he looked almost like a college professor. "That's Dean Turner?" Joe asked Chet in a whisper.

Chet shrugged. "I guess so. I've never met him. I've only seen his picture in the Circus U. catalog."

"He's not exactly the kind of guy you'd expect to be shot from a cannon, is he?" Frank asked Joe.

The crowd grew quiet as the dean began to speak. "I'd like to welcome you all here today. I'm Paul Turner, dean of Circus University and a member of the board of directors of the Montero Brothers Circus. We're very proud to have you here for this annual open house. Bayport has always welcomed the circus and Circus U., and we're glad to have this chance to thank you."

For the next few minutes, Turner explained the purpose of Circus U. for the crowd of students and Bayport residents. At the end of his speech, he told them, "Please feel free to stay and watch the circus performers rehearse, and to ask the students and performers whatever questions you have. There will be circus performances all week, and I hope you will want to attend at least one." Dean Turner smiled. "The performance Friday night should be particularly exciting, because the Bayport High students will be performing along with the circus performers."

A buzz of excitement ran through the audience. Frank and Joe turned and looked at Chet. "Did you know that was going to happen?" Joe whispered.

Chet nodded and smiled happily. "And you guys had better be there."

"And now, without further ado," Dean Turner continued, "I'd like to show you all a trick I used to perform back in my professional circus days, before I became the dean at Circus U."

"I can't believe he's going to get in that cannon with his tweed jacket on," Joe said.

But Turner had stepped back from the podium and removed his jacket. He rolled up the sleeves of his shirt and straightened his bow tie. Nearby, a man in a tuxedo sitting at a drum set began to play a snare drum. Turner bowed to the audience and walked slowly toward the cannon.

"That's one of the things I love about the circus," Joe whispered. "The suspense."

"Shh," Chet said. "I can't concentrate."

When Turner reached the ladder that led up to the cannon's mouth, he turned to the crowd.

"Don't try this at home," he joked. "This stunt requires special training. The kind of training a place like Circus U. offers, in fact."

He turned and began to climb the ladder. When he got to the top, he grabbed the rim of the cannon and hoisted himself feetfirst into the barrel. Two men in circus blazers removed the ladder. Then a tall woman with long brown hair stepped across the ring to the end of the cannon. A long fuse reached out of the cannon and trailed to the ground. The woman lit the fuse with a flourish, and it began to burn, sending out sparks.

Next to him, Joe heard Chet draw in his breath. He glanced over at his friend. Chet was sitting on the edge of the bleacher, watching every move. As the fuse came closer to the cannon, Chet's eyes widened.

Then, in a flash, the fuse went off, lighting the gunpowder inside the cannon. A huge boom exploded from the barrel, and smoke came pouring out.

The crowd let out a gasp. Joe waited to see Turner shoot from the cannon's barrel, but nothing happened. More and more smoke appeared, but there was still no sign of the dean.

Then he heard the sound of coughing coming from the cannon and Dean Turner's voice cry out, "Help! Someone help me!"

4 The Disappearing Juggler

Frank jumped up from his seat and raced down the aisle ahead of Joe and Chet. As he hurried across the ring to the cannon, he heard Dean Turner's cries for help grow weaker and weaker.

"Help him!" a man in the audience shouted. "He'll suffocate in there!"

Frank saw that the man was right. Smoke was pouring out of the cannon's mouth now, filling the area with a smelly, bluish haze.

The tall woman who had lit the fuse was standing by the cannon, a worried expression on her face. Frank quickly tried to think of a plan. The cannon was a good ten feet above the ground.

"Help," Turner said faintly. "I can't last much . . ."

At that moment, Joe and Chet came up to Frank. "What's the matter?" Joe asked. "Why can't he get out by himself?"

"I think he's been overcome by smoke," Frank said. He coughed and added, "We've got to think of a way to get him out of there—fast."

He fanned the smoke away from his face, coughing several times as huge billows kept pouring out of the cannon. Joe was rubbing his eyes, and Chet had his hand over his mouth.

Frank motioned for Joe to hold back the crowd that had formed around them. A short, wiry older man stood by, scowling. "Do something, boys," he snapped. "Or let someone else take over."

"Why don't *you* do something," Joe muttered angrily.

Chet grabbed Joe's arm. "That's Bo Costello, director of admissions at Circus U.," he told Joe in a harsh whisper. "Keep cool."

"Joe, Chet," Frank called out suddenly. "Get the ladder Dean Turner used to get into the cannon. Hurry!"

Seconds later, Joe and Chet returned with the ladder. They propped it up against the mouth of the cannon and held it in place as Frank scrambled up the rungs.

The smoke had thinned out a little. When

32

Frank reached the cannon's mouth, he could see Turner lying on his stomach deep inside the cannon. Frank desperately hoped the dean was still conscious. He stretched his arm down into the dark barrel.

"Dean Turner, can you reach my hand?" he asked. There was no reply. Frank waited an anxious moment, then he felt Turner's fingers meet his. "Hold tight," Frank said. "I'm going to pull you out."

He glanced down and saw that his brother and Chet were holding the ladder securely. Frank leaned into the barrel and pulled Dean Turner's hand—hard.

Frank coughed at the trails of smoke that kept coming out of the barrel. "On three," he said. "One. Two. Three." Frank put all his strength into his grip and pulled. He felt Turner come sliding toward him. Frank stepped down two rungs and pulled the dean out of the cannon. Turner was shaking, but he slowly made his way down the ladder with Frank behind him.

When they reached the floor, Frank led Dean Turner over to a seat in the first row. A tall man hurried over to them, carrying a portable oxygen tank.

"I'm the circus doctor," he told Frank. "I'll take over now. Do you need some oxygen?"

Frank shook his head and stepped away. He took a few deep breaths and began to feel better.

"Nice work," Joe said, coming up to him. "Maybe the circus could feature you in one of their acts—'Frank Hardy, the daredevil rescuer.'" Then he looked at his brother and added in a serious tone, "You sure you're okay, Frank?"

"I'm fine," Frank replied. "I just hope Dean Turner's okay."

The Hardys walked over to where Dean Turner was sitting. He was holding an oxygen mask over his face. When the dean saw Frank, he removed the mask and smiled. "Thank you, young man," he said. "You saved my life."

"I'm just glad you're all right," Frank said. The dean nodded, then sat back in his chair and closed his eyes. Frank turned to Joe. "Let's find out what happened to that cannon."

As soon as Frank and Joe reached the cannon, Chet came up to them. He was carrying a fire extinguisher. "I found it backstage," he told them, handing the extinguisher to Frank.

"Good work," Frank said. "Hold the ladder again." He took the extinguisher from Chet and climbed up the ladder. When he got to the top, Frank squirted the foam inside the cannon at what was left of the smoke. Frank leaned into the cannon's mouth and sniffed. He was sure he smelled oil. That would have caused the blue haze that had formed out of the smoke, he thought. He climbed down and told Joe what he had discovered.

34

"Oil, sure," Joe said, after he had made the climb up to the cannon. "I feel it, too," he added, showing Frank a greasy finger. "But there's more," he added. "I smell gasoline, and unless I'm wrong, there are traces of gunpowder inside here, too."

"Someone wanted this thing to blow," Frank said as Joe climbed back down. "They must have known that with the fuse lit, the gasoline would ignite, blowing up the gunpowder."

"And the oil was probably thrown in to make the fire more smoky," Joe finished.

"We've got to tell Dean Turner about this," Chet said, a worried expression on his face.

"Let's wait until he's recovered," Frank suggested. The crowd that had gathered around the dean was starting to thin out. Bo Costello was telling the audience that refreshments were being served in the foyer.

As the crowd left, Frank noticed that the tall, brown-haired woman was sitting next to Turner and speaking to him in a loud voice. He inched closer to hear what she was saying.

"Now are you going to listen to me?" she was asking in a high voice. "What more is it going to take before you do something?"

"Georgianne," Turner said, wiping his grimy face with a large white handkerchief, "please don't start in on me again. It was an accident."

"Like the one last week in Atlanta, when the

tiger got out of his cage? Or two days ago when the prop room caught on fire? It's a miracle nobody's been hurt. When are you going to realize that these aren't just accidents?" she demanded.

Frank motioned to Joe and Chet and whispered to them what he had just overheard. "It looks like Circus U. has had more than its share of accidents lately," he said.

Chet's eyes widened. "Whew," he said, letting out a long breath. "You think it's sabotage?"

"Hard to say," Joe said with a shrug. "But we should definitely tell Dean Turner about the gasoline. Especially if this isn't the first time something's gone wrong at Circus U."

The three of them walked up to Dean Turner. "Feeling better?" Frank asked, taking in the man's sooty face and dirty clothes.

"I'm fine now," Dean Turner said, smiling. "Thanks to you."

Frank paused for a moment. "There's something you should know," he said finally. He told the dean about finding traces of oil and gasoline in the barrel. "It looks like someone wanted you to go up in smoke," Frank finished.

The brown-haired woman stared at Frank, then turned and faced Dean Turner. "See. I told you so. If this so-called accident doesn't make you take action, then I will!" With that, she got up from her seat and stormed off.

"You'll have to excuse my assistant," Turner said as he watched her leave. "She can be temperamental."

"What did she mean by 'so-called accident'?" Joe asked.

Turner sighed. "Georgianne Unger—that's my assistant's name—thinks that some recent mishaps during the circus's tour are more than just accidents."

"Like what just happened in the cannon?" Chet offered.

"Exactly." Turner reached for his jacket, took his glasses out of the pocket, and put them on. "That's better. Now at least I can see you boys. Paul Turner," he said, reaching out his hand.

"Frank Hardy," Frank said, shaking Turner's hand. "This is my brother, Joe, and our friend Chet Morton. Chet's taking classes at Circus U."

A big smile appeared on Turner's face. "That's great," he said to Chet. "I just hope this little event hasn't spoiled your love for the circus."

Chet shook his head vigorously. "Not a chance."

"Good," Turner said. "I'm glad to hear it."

At that moment, Bo Costello came over with a younger man and a woman in tow. The man had short brown hair and was dressed in jeans and a flannel shirt. The woman was blond and short, and she wore a red, white, and blue Circus U. warm-up suit. Both looked to be in their early twenties. "Turner, we've got to talk," Costello said. "These students are very concerned about this latest incident, as you might guess. Some of the circus performers have spoken to me, too."

"You've got to do something before someone gets seriously hurt," the woman urged.

"We're all getting nervous," the man added. The man's smooth drawl sounded familiar to Frank. Then he realized who the man was: Carl Nash. Without his clown makeup, Frank hadn't recognized Nash at first. The Circus U. student gave the Hardys and Chet a nod of recognition.

"Carl Nash and Justine Leone speak for all the students, I think," Costello went on, "when they express their worries about what has been happening. As dean of Circus U. and the manager of this tour of the Montero Brothers Circus, it is up to you to take action."

Turner sighed and ran his hands through his hair. "Okay, Bo. I get the message."

Costello stood with his hands on his hips, his small, wiry frame obviously tense. "We can't keep having these accidents," he insisted.

"Okay, okay." Turner sighed in exasperation. "Relax, Bo. I'm sorry, Carl, Justine," he added, turning to the students with a concerned look. "We'll get to the bottom of this. I promise."

Frank saw Nash's eyes brighten a little and a smile appear on his face. But Justine gave Bo an insistent look.

Bo responded to the look by saying to Turner, "If anything else goes wrong, I'm going to be the first one to call the trustees of Circus U. and the board of directors of the circus. I'll even beat Georgianne to the punch. You can count on it."

With that, Costello walked off, followed closely by Justine and Nash.

"What did he mean by 'beat Georgianne to the punch'?" Frank asked Turner.

The dean smiled nervously. "Georgianne has been threatening to call the trustees and board members to tell them about the mishaps we've been having."

"And you don't want them to know," Joe concluded.

"I'd rather they didn't, until I know for certain that it's something serious," Turner admitted, gazing ahead at the three rings and the circus apparatus in them. He faced the Hardys and Chet with a look of concern and embarrassment. "I might get kicked off the board, and the trustees may decide I'm not competent enough to run Circus U."

"You think they might fire you as dean?" Frank asked.

Turner sighed. "They could." He paused, then went on. "You have to realize that the circus is my life. I've loved performing in it, and I love teaching young people who want to be performers." He shook his head. "I don't know what I'd do if I couldn't be part of the circus anymore."

"Maybe what you need are detectives to help you figure out why you've been having trouble here lately," Chet said. He smiled and pointed to Frank and Joe. "And I've got the perfect detectives for you."

"You two are detectives?" Turner asked, raising an eyebrow.

Frank nodded. "We've solved a few cases around town," he said.

"Frank's just being modest," Chet said. "He and Joe have solved mysteries that even the police couldn't figure out."

Turner rubbed his chin thoughtfully. "Well, I'm not sure there's anything to investigate, really," he said. "But maybe if you keep your eyes open you might notice something."

"You want us to look around?" Joe asked.

Turner paused for a moment, then he said slowly, "Not officially. But if we gave you special admittance here, you could attend classes and be around just in case there is another accident."

"Special admittance?" Frank asked. "You mean we'd be students here?"

"That's right," Turner said with a nod.

"That's a great idea," Chet said with excitement. "You can come to my clowning class." He glanced at his watch. "It's in five minutes."

"Well, okay," Joe said. "But no way will I put on a clown costume."

Turner shook Frank's hand. "Good. I'm happy to have you boys admitted as special students of Circus U. Look around and tell me if you see anything suspicious."

"We will," Joe assured him.

"Now, if you'll excuse me," Turner said, "I have to change these clothes and get back to work." With that, Dean Turner gave the three boys a nod and headed across the arena.

"All right!" Chet cried, slapping Frank on the back. "Welcome aboard. Let's go. We don't want to be late for clowning class."

"Not so fast," Frank said. "We still need to find out about our mystery juggler."

"Sorry, Chet," Joe added. "We'll have to skip our first class."

"That's not very responsible of you," Chet said with a smile. "But okay. Come by later and pick me up. We can grab lunch."

"Sounds good," Frank said as Chet went off.

"Be careful," Joe called out after him. "Clowning's serious business."

Chet laughed and broke into a run. When he was gone, Frank faced his brother and said, "Ready to find our mystery juggler?"

Joe nodded. "Where should we start?"

Frank looked over at the rings. "Let's talk to

some people with the Montero Brothers Circus. Chances are, the mystery juggler is a full-time performer with the circus."

"He could have been a Circus U. student," Joe pointed out.

"True," Frank agreed. "But we have to start somewhere."

Several minutes later, Frank and Joe had sneaked past a guard and taken the elevator down to the bottom floor. Even though it was still early, the floor was alive with activity. The double doors to the animal room were open, and the Hardys could see groomers feeding seals and washing a baby elephant. Performers were bustling in and out of the dressing rooms. Frank asked a circus performer wearing a leotard and sweatpants where he might find the clowns. The woman directed him to a rehearsal room down the hall. She called it "clown alley."

"Clown alley," Joe said, laughing. "That's funny."

"Chet told me that the circus clowns always stake out a room where they hang out together and rehearse," Frank said. "The clowns' room came to be known as clown alley." He led the way down the hall in the direction the woman had pointed. Soon they came to a large room that contained dressing tables and a rack hung with clown costumes. Several men and women, some in costumes and some in street clothes, were standing around the room, drinking cups of coffee and talking to each other.

"Excuse me," Frank said, stepping into the room. "Can I ask you a few questions?"

A red-haired man in jeans and a Montero Brothers Circus T-shirt looked Frank over. "About what?" he wanted to know.

Frank introduced himself and Joe to the man, who said his name was Jim Jacobs. Frank described the mystery juggler to Jacobs. "Does he sound familiar to you?" Frank asked. "Someone with the circus, maybe?"

Jacobs nodded. "Yeah," he said. "I know exactly who you're talking about. There's only one guy around here who wears baggy green-striped pants."

Frank felt his excitement growing. He exchanged a look with Joe. Now they were getting somewhere.

"Funny you should be searching for him, though," Jacobs went on, looking at the brothers curiously.

"Why's that?" Frank asked.

"Because I am, too," Jacobs explained. "I had an appointment with him after the performance last night, but he didn't show up. And nobody's seen him this morning. The guy you're looking for has totally disappeared!"

5 Chet Takes a Giant Step

"He's disappeared?" Joe asked in disbelief.

"That's right," Jacobs said. "We've checked his motel room, and everyone's been looking for him for the past two hours. The guy's gone!"

Joe kicked the floor in frustration. "There goes our only lead."

"Not necessarily," Frank said. "The guy could turn up."

"I wouldn't be so sure," Jacobs said. "Ralph Rosen—that's the guy's name—pulls these disappearing acts a lot. And when he's gone, he's gone." Jacobs let out a whistle and made a sweeping gesture with his hand. "Adios, amigos. We're not gonna be seeing him around here again. I never should have hired him."

"If you knew about these disappearing acts, why did you hire him in the first place?" Frank asked.

Jacobs shrugged his shoulders. "Who knows? When you're head clown like I am, you take who's good, and he was good, that's for sure. I have to admit that before I hired him for this tour, I'd heard he was pretty unreliable about showing up for rehearsals and performances. But I needed a good juggling act, and Rosen needed the job." He paused and looked intently at the Hardys. "Why are you looking for him, anyway? What did you mean just now when you said he was your only lead? And who let you back here? This area is for circus personnel only."

Joe saw Frank's warning look and thought quickly. "We're part-time students at Circus U. He was doing a trick last night that my brother and I wanted to learn. That's all we wanted."

Jacobs laughed. Joe was relieved to see he believed their story. "Which trick?" Jacobs asked. "I bet I could show you."

"Umm . . . the one with the . . ." Joe was stumped. He tried to remember something special about what the juggler had been doing the night before.

Frank came to the rescue. "What my brother meant to say was that we know how to juggle a little," he said, "but Rosen kept five balls in the air. Joe and I thought he might give us a lead on how to handle more than three."

"That's easy," Jacobs said. Before Joe could say another word, Jacobs dashed over to a dressing table and came back with five tennis balls. "If you can do three, you can do as many as you want," he explained, tossing the balls in the air one by one. "The principle's exactly the same."

One after another, Jacobs tossed all five balls in the air. Grabbing a ball with his right hand, he tossed it back into the air as his left hand grabbed another. "You try it," he said, passing a ball to Joe as it came down.

Joe jumped as Jacobs shot him the ball. He hadn't expected to have to juggle for the man. Before he could react, Jacobs had tossed him another, and another, and Joe was hurling them up into the air as fast as Jacobs threw them. With no time to think, Joe had all five balls going at once and was frantically shuffling them back into the air as fast as they landed.

"You've got it!" Jacobs shouted. "There you go. All right."

"Way to go, Joe," Frank added.

"Keep your eyes on them," Jacobs said.

As soon as Jacobs directed him, Joe began to think about what he was doing, and he faltered. One by one, he dropped the balls. Soon they were all bouncing and rolling on the ground.

Joe looked at his brother. Frank's expression was a mixture of amusement and sympathy. "You almost had it," he said, barely holding back a smile. "Next time, don't think."

"Let's see you try," Joe said, passing the balls to Frank.

"No thanks," Frank said, holding up one hand. "I'll pass on this one."

"Come on, Frank," Joe urged. "Just do it."

"Your brother here almost had the hang of it," Jacobs said.

Frank shook his head. "We've got a class to go to."

"Chicken," Joe whispered under his breath. Then he said to Jacobs, "Thanks for the lesson."

"No problem," Jacobs said. "Come back any time."

"We'll do that," Joe told him as they walked away. "Thanks for setting me up like that, Frank. You're a real pal."

Frank grinned at his brother. "You did pretty well. I didn't know you could juggle."

Joe smiled wryly. "Neither did I. It's amazing what you can do when you try." He ran his hands through his blond hair and thought for a moment. "With Rosen gone, this case is shot."

"Not necessarily." Frank counted off on his fingers. "One, the guy might turn up. From what Jacobs said, it sounds like he needs this job. Two, we still have the code to crack. And three, there's the sabotage to investigate. We're not out of the business yet."

"Leave it to Frank Hardy to look on the bright side. Come on. We'd better get to Chet's class."

Frank nodded. "And after class, I think we should ask Dean Turner some more questions about the sabotage. And I want to talk to his assistant, Georgianne Unger, too."

The Hardys made their way toward the prop classroom Chet had shown them earlier. There was a sign on the door that read Clowning in Session. Through the glass pane Joe spotted Chet along with the other clowning students. Joe eased the door open and, being careful not to disturb the class, he and Frank stepped inside.

The classroom was large, with a high ceiling and bright lights. Along one wall there were workbenches set up with all kinds of materials, including wood, Styrofoam, and paint. Joe remembered what Chet had told him about the clowns making their own props.

The class was concentrating on stilt-walking. Ten students were gathered around Paul Turner, who was up on ten-foot-high stilts and walking smoothly around the room.

"I didn't expect him to teach these classes," Joe said.

"You mean the dean?" Frank asked.

Joe nodded. "He's good, too. Just don't volunteer me for this stunt, okay?"

Before Frank could answer, Turner had jumped off the stilts and was speaking to the class. "No clown walks on stilts this high right away," he said. "That would be like a baby running before it could walk." The class laughed nervously as Turner went over to some shorter stilts that were leaning against a wall. "We start with these," he said, holding up a pair of five-foot-high stilts. "Who wants to go first?"

Joe waited for someone in the class to volunteer. No one raised his hand. Then Chet's hand shot up. "I can't believe it," Joe said to Frank. "Chet's a great football player, but I can't see him mastering a skill like this. The only other time he got up on stilts, he fell off them."

"He can handle it," Frank said. "Chet may be big, but he's not clumsy."

"We'll see," Joe said. With Turner's help, Chet stepped onto the stilts.

"The trick here," Turner explained to the class, "is to pretend these sticks are just another part of your legs. They won't bend," he said. "And they won't break, either."

"I sure hope not," Chet said, taking a small step.

Joe held his breath, then let it out slowly as Turner let go of the stilts. Chet started moving around the room. He wobbled and the stilts started shaking under him. With every step he took it looked as if he might fall, but then he began to get the hang of it.

"Hey," Joe said, watching Chet walk around the room. "He's not bad."

"I told you," Frank countered.

As soon as the words were out of Frank's mouth, he heard a yell. Frank and Joe looked over and saw Chet swaying back and forth. Several members of the class let out a gasp. One woman held her hand to her mouth.

"Chet!" Joe shouted, rushing toward his friend.

But before Joe could reach him, he saw the stilt under Chet's right leg snap in half. It broke in two, and Chet fell to the ground in a heap.

6 Dean Turner's Dilemma

"Chet!" Frank called out, following his brother to where Chet was lying on the floor. "Are you all right?"

As Joe was pulling Chet up, Paul Turner rushed over to them. "I'm so sorry," he said. "I should have been spotting you better."

"That's okay," Chet answered, rubbing his elbow and grimacing. "I just fell on my funny bone, that's all."

The rest of the class had crowded around, looking at Chet to make sure he wasn't hurt.

Dean Turner turned to them and announced, "It's okay, everybody. Can you all please stand back and give us a little room?"

The class edged back a bit, and Frank put his arm around Chet. "Are you sure you're all right?" he asked in a concerned tone.

Chet nodded silently, but his face turned slightly red. "It's a little embarrassing," he confessed as he slowly got to his feet. "I mean, these stilts weren't exactly tall."

"You're not the first clown to take a fall," Turner told him, a smile crossing his face. "And you won't be the last."

"Dean Turner's right," Joe said reassuringly. "What's more important is that you're okay."

Frank spotted the stilts lying on the ground next to Chet. The sight of one of them, split clean in half, made him wonder. What if Chet's accident was another example of the sabotage at the circus?

Frank went over to the broken stilt and picked it up. A quick glance at it confirmed his suspicion. The stilt had obviously been sawn halfway through.

"Hey, Joe," he called out to his brother. "Check this out."

Joe came over, Chet at his side. When Joe took one look at the stilt, he let out a low whistle. "This was no accident," he said. "That stilt's been sawn partially through."

Chet's eyes widened with fear. He swallowed hard as he stared at the stilt. "You mean someone wanted that stilt to snap in half?" he asked in a shaky voice.

"That's right, Chet," Frank said grimly, examining the saw mark.

"Is something wrong, boys?" Dean Turner asked, appearing at Frank's side.

Frank nodded. "I'm afraid there is," he said, showing the stilt to Turner and pointing out the saw mark. Frank saw a flash of alarm pass over the dean's face, but Turner recovered quickly and turned to the class.

"We've almost reached the end of our class time," he said, checking his watch. "I'm going to dismiss you early so you can have a short break before your next class."

As the class filed out, Turner faced Frank. "This was no accident," he concluded. "But who could have done this?" he added in a desperate tone. "And why?"

"Don't worry, Dean Turner," Chet said. "Frank and Joe will find out."

"Thanks for the vote of confidence," Joe muttered.

"Who had access to these stilts?" Frank asked, pointing to them.

"I collected them myself from the prop room this morning," Turner told him. "Before my speech. I didn't notice anything wrong with them then," he added weakly.

"So they were in here the whole time you were making your speech?" Joe asked.

"I assume so," Turner said. "But I really can't be sure."

"And could anyone have come into the class-room during that time?" Frank asked.

"That's right," Turner said softly. He looked at the broken stilt and shook his head. "Oh, this is terrible. I just don't know what to do."

"Maybe you could help us come up with a solid lead," Joe said firmly. "Like the name of some-one who might have a reason to cause these accidents."

Turner sighed. "I can't think of anyone off-hand. Look, I have to go back to my office now. I'm expecting a very important phone call. Why don't you boys come by in a few minutes? We can sit down and talk at length about these inci-dents."

"Good idea," Frank said. "I know my brother and I have a lot of questions to ask."

"Like what?" Chet asked.

"Well, Dean Turner still hasn't told us how the other accidents happened," Frank said. "We need to know all the facts before we can start to narrow in on a list of suspects."

"Oh, I really don't like that word," Turner said, shaking his head sadly. " 'Suspects' sounds so— so criminal. I just cannot believe there's some kind of criminal running around here trying to sabotage the circus. In fact, I refuse to believe it."

"But you've just seen evidence that points to sabotage," Frank said, trying not to sound impatient. The dean was a nice man, Frank thought, but he didn't seem to have a clue about what was going on right under his nose.

"Your assistant said no one had gotten hurt," Joe said. "But the next victim might not be so lucky. He or she might get more than a lungful of smoke or a bruised elbow."

The dean looked at them for a moment. Then he nodded abruptly and said, "All right. Come to my office and we'll talk." He turned and headed out of the classroom.

"Well," Chet said, watching the dean walk away, "I hate to leave you guys in the lurch like this, but I have to take off, too. I'm going to be late for my clown makeup class."

"You sure you're okay?" Frank asked him.

Chet rubbed his elbow and laughed a little. "I'm fine, really. You want to have lunch when my class is over?" he asked.

"Sure," Frank said, knowing how much his friend liked to eat. In fact, he was amazed that Chet had gone this long without stopping to grab a bite. "We'll meet you in the arena after your class. What time?"

"About an hour and a half," Chet said, turning toward the door. "And good luck."

"We're going to need it," Frank said. "Especially at the rate we're going."

"Yeah," Joe agreed. "First the juggler disappears, then it turns out our list of suspects for the person who cut that stilt in half includes everyone appearing in the Montero Brothers Circus, plus the students at Circus U."

"The only people we can rule out are the Bayport High students," Frank said. "Because the incidents started before the circus arrived in Bayport." He headed for the door. "Let's go talk to Turner. He's got to have some idea of who might be out to get him, or the circus."

"I hope so," Joe agreed, starting off down the hall.

"You know where we're going?" Frank asked.

"Sure," Joe said, as he turned right at the elevators. "Remember this morning Chet said this is where the Circus U. offices were?"

Frank nodded as he followed Joe. They passed by a door marked with Georgianne Unger's name. Next to it was Bo Costello's office. A little farther down the hall, Joe found a door with Dean Turner's name on it.

The dean had just hung up the phone when Frank and Joe reached the doorway. Turner looked up and motioned to the Hardys to come in.

"Sit down," Turner said, indicating two chairs that faced the desk. "I was just on the phone with one of our Circus U. donors. He wanted to have his name put on a bleacher in our big top in

Florida." Turner laughed and raised his eyebrows. "I suggested he might want to contribute more money and have a whole classroom with his name on it."

Frank smiled. "Let's talk about possible suspects, Dean Turner," he said, getting right to the point. "Can you think of anyone who might want to ruin your reputation? After all, you're not only dean of Circus U., but you're also managing the Montero Brothers Circus tour this year."

Turner paused for a moment. Then he said, "I hate to suggest this, but Georgianne is a good possibility."

"Georgianne Unger?" Joe asked, remembering the name on the door they'd passed. "You mean your assistant?"

Turner nodded and went on. "She's not only my assistant. She's also a former circus performer and teaches makeup classes at Circus U.," Turner explained.

"Why do you think she might be responsible?" Frank asked.

"Well, for one thing, the first incident took place in her class," Turner replied.

"Tell us about it," Joe said, leaning forward in his chair.

"It happened about six months ago in Florida. Apparently the clown face makeup the students in Georgianne's class were using made them break out in a terrible rash. It didn't seem significant at the time, until some other things started happening."

"Like the tiger getting loose and the prop room catching on fire," Frank offered, remembering the conversation he'd overheard between Turner and his assistant.

Turner nodded slowly. "Exactly. But before that happened, there was also a small explosion in one of Bo Costello's classes."

"What do you mean by a small explosion?" Joe asked.

"Bo was outside, teaching his students about fireworks," Turner continued. "Some circuses use small fireworks displays to keep the crowds entertained during scene changes. Anyway," he went on with a small shrug, "there was a small uncontrolled explosion. Maybe the students weren't being properly supervised, although Bo insists that wasn't the case. Anyway, no one was hurt. End of story."

"And the tiger getting loose?" Frank asked, storing up the information about the explosion. "How did that happen?"

"Another visiting circus that was passing through Atlanta lent us a tiger—a trained tiger, mind you," Turner said. "The keeper failed to secure its cage, and it got loose. It was quite a scene, as you can imagine, but we quickly captured the animal."

"And the prop room?" Joe asked.

"The fire department investigated, and they concluded that someone had left oily rags and sawdust too close to some gasoline," Turner replied. "A cigarette butt may have been the cause of the fire. I dismissed the prop manager, and we haven't had another problem."

"Until today with Chet's stilts," Frank pointed out.

Turner was silent for a moment. "As you yourself suggested, anyone could have gone into the classroom and sawn through that stilt. I'm very sorry for what happened to your friend, though," he added softly.

"But you think Georgianne might be behind these accidents, as you call them," Frank said.

"It's possible," Turner said finally. He leaned forward in his chair and looked at the Hardys intently. "You want my honest opinion? I suspect that she wants my job and my seat on the board of directors of the Montero Brothers Circus. A seat on the board is an honor that comes with the deanship. Georgianne hopes these accidents will cause the trustees and the board to fire me and replace me with her. But what she doesn't realize is that it will never happen."

"Why not?" Joe asked.

"Because she's too young and too inexperienced. If anyone is going to replace me, it will be an experienced circus performer getting ready to retire, or a longtime member of the Circus U. faculty, like Bo Costello. He's been with Circus U. almost as long as I have."

"Does Ms. Unger know this?" Frank asked.

"Not as far as I can tell." Turner rubbed his forehead. "I'd hate to believe it was Georgianne, anyway. I know she appears to be ambitious and all, but I've worked with her long enough to know that she's also got a heart of gold." He stood up from his chair. "Is there anything else I can help you with?" he asked. "I hate to cut this short, but I do have a lot of work."

"Just one more question," Frank said.

"Yes?" Dean Turner asked.

"Why hasn't Georgianne called the trustees yet to tell them about all these accidents?" Frank asked.

Turner shook his head and shrugged. "I don't know. She keeps threatening, but so far she hasn't followed through on her threats."

"That seems a little strange, doesn't it?" Joe asked. "Since, as you say, she wants your job."

Frank nodded in agreement. "But who knows. Maybe she's waiting for someone to get hurt, so it looks really bad."

"I hope not," Turner said sadly. "That's a terrible thought."

The Hardys had just gotten up from their chairs when the phone on Turner's desk rang.

60

Turner answered it. Frank motioned to Joe that they should leave.

Turner held his hand over the mouthpiece and said, "Please, boys, stay a moment, if you don't mind."

Frank exchanged a look with Joe and sat back down in the chair across from Turner's desk. The dean didn't say more than two or three words to the person on the other end of the line. After a moment he hung up the phone and sat down slowly, a dazed expression on his face.

"What is it?" Joe asked.

"What's wrong?" Frank said.

"That was the head trustee for Circus U.," Turner said dully.

"And?" Frank asked.

Turner swallowed before going on. "He said that Georgianne Unger just called him to tell him about the accidents. He said that unless I find out who is behind the incidents within one week, I'll be removed as dean of Circus U."

7 A Coded Connection

"What?" Joe asked Turner. "You mean they'll fire you?"

"That's exactly what I mean," Turner said. He rounded his desk and started pacing back and forth. "Oh, this is terrible, just terrible."

Joe watched as Frank stepped over to Turner and put his hand on the dean's arm. "Calm down," the older Hardy urged. "We'll get to the bottom of this."

"Frank's right, Dean Turner," Joe put in. "We've got a week. That's plenty of time."

Turner sighed deeply. "Oh, I hope so," he said. "Oh, no," he added, looking at his watch. "I have an appointment with an important donor in fifteen minutes. Would you mind—"

"No problem," Joe said. "There's just one more question. What do you know about a guy with the Montero Brothers Circus by the name of Ralph Rosen?"

Dean Turner looked puzzled. "Ralph Rosen? I personally kicked him out of this school about a year ago."

"You mean Rosen went to Circus U.?" Joe asked.

"He did," Turner said. "Until he got expelled. In fact, I'm stunned to hear that he's working for the Montero Brothers Circus. Jim Jacobs didn't tell me he'd hired him. I'll have to speak to him about that. With his record, Rosen shouldn't even be clowning for a third-rate outfit, let alone a world-class circus like the Montero." Turner shook his head a few times, as if trying to clear his thoughts. "How did you find out that Rosen was working for the circus?"

"It's a long story," Joe said. He took a deep breath and quickly explained to Dean Turner that Rosen had dropped one of his juggler's balls in Chet's tote bag and then disappeared. "So we went looking for him," he went on. "But the guy's taken off."

"I'm not surprised," Turner said. "About Rosen taking off, that is. He used to miss classes all the time. When he did come he would disrupt the entire class. He was a terrific juggler, but he had a terrible attitude. He thought he was better than everyone, and he wouldn't take direction. Costello wanted me to give him a break. He said Rosen had a lot of talent and just needed the proper guidance, but in the end he was forced to agree with my decision to dismiss him. Circus U. was not the place for someone like Ralph Rosen."

"That guy we talked to—what was his name?" Frank asked his brother.

"Jim Jacobs," Joe replied, "the head clown."

"Right," Frank said. "Jim Jacobs admitted Rosen had a bad reputation, but he said he felt sorry for him. Rosen was juggling on the street for money, apparently."

Turner shrugged. "I'm not surprised. With his attitude, it's unlikely any circus would hire him. Although you don't need a degree from Circus U. to be qualified to work in circuses," he added.

"Is there any way we can find out more about Ralph Rosen?" Frank asked.

"You should ask Bo," Turner replied. "He would have a record of his application. And Jacobs will know where he's staying in Bayport. I'm still not sure why you want to find him, though. What was so important about that ball he dropped in your friend's bag?"

Joe pulled a piece of paper out of his pocket and showed Turner the coded message. "This was inside the ball," he explained, handing over the slip of paper.

After Turner scanned the paper, he glanced up

at Joe with a questioning look in his eyes. "Do you have any idea what this means?" he asked.

Before Joe could answer, Frank spoke up. "Actually, we don't."

From the dean's expression, Joe could tell Turner had an idea. "Why, do you?" Joe asked.

"These letters popped out at me right away," Turner explained. "Of course they mean more to me than to you, since I know these people."

"What do you mean?" Joe asked, frustrated at Turner for taking so long to get to the point. "What people?"

Turner pointed to the paper. "CN, JL, and GU are all initials of people at the circus."

"They are?" Joe grabbed the paper from Turner and looked at it again.

"Carl Nash, Justine Leone—" Turner said.

"And Georgianne Unger," Frank finished. "Boy, are we dense."

"Not really. We only just met these people," Joe reminded his brother. "But I have to admit, I do feel pretty stupid for not noticing the connection before." He stared at the numbers that went along with the letters. "The question is, what do these numbers mean?"

"And why are these initials on this list?" Frank added, looking over his brother's shoulder.

"Well, you boys are the detectives," Turner said, shrugging.

Joe pocketed the slip of paper and headed for

the door. "We'll take it from here," he told Turner. "If you think of anything else that might be helpful—"

"I'll let you know," Turner said. He crossed the room and held the door open for them. "Good luck to you two, and thanks again for what you're doing. I can't tell you how much I appreciate it."

"No problem," Frank said.

"We'll keep you posted," Joe added, closing the door behind them. He followed Frank into the hallway.

"So now we know that Ralph Rosen once attended Circus U.," Frank said.

"And he was kicked out," Joe added. "Think he has a grudge against Turner? Enough of a grudge to have caused the problems at Circus U. and the circus here?"

"It's a possibility," Frank admitted. "But how does that tie in to the coded message he passed to Chet?" He bit his lip in frustration. "We need to find out more about Ralph Rosen."

"Let's ask Costello. Maybe he can help us out." Joe waited while a student walked down the hall past them before going on. "So we're back to where we started. We know who Rosen is, but we don't know how to find him. We think the code may refer to people here at the circus, but we don't know why." Joe tried to sort out all the details in his mind. "Hey," he said. "I just thought of something."

"What?" Frank said. "I recognize that look. You're about to make a flying leap at deduction."

"That's what makes me such a good detective," Joe said, pointing his finger at Frank's chest. "Let's say the code is somehow related to the sabotage."

"We don't know that for sure," Frank warned.

"No, we don't," Joe admitted. "But let's just say it is."

"Okay," Frank said slowly. "What then?"

Joe searched for a connection he just knew had to be there. "Say Rosen is connected to the sabotage," he said. "He gets kicked out of Circus U. and decides to get even with Turner, out of revenge," Joe explained in a rush. "Maybe the code was some kind of note he was passing to an accomplice, someone on the inside who was helping him for their own reasons. They could be working together."

Joe waited for his brother to respond. "Well?" Joe asked finally, when Frank had kept quiet for too long.

"I see your point," Frank said slowly. "But why would Rosen need to pass information to his accomplice? Why not just make phone calls? Remember, the sabotage started before Circus U. and the Montero Circus ever got to Bayport. Also, why would his accomplice take instructions from Rosen?"

"I don't know," Joe said in exasperation. "That's what we have to find out. You got a better idea?" Joe raised his eyebrows and waited for his brother's response.

"Hey, don't be so defensive," Frank said.

"I'm not defensive," Joe said. "It's just that when you don't have any ideas, you want to shoot down mine."

"I'm not shooting them down," Frank explained. "I'm just trying to see if they make sense. Let's go meet Chet and get some lunch. We can grab a burger and go over what we know."

"Sure," Joe said, still feeling that Frank wasn't taking his idea seriously. He decided to find some proof to back up his deduction.

"You know," Joe said as he and Frank started walking down the hall toward the elevators, "Rosen could be working with Carl Nash. Remember last night when Carl showed up? He was wearing the same costume as Chet. What if Rosen meant to pass the message to Nash?"

Frank turned to his brother. "Now you're onto something. Why didn't we think of that before?"

"What if Nash is Rosen's accomplice?" Joe pressed.

"Why would his initials be on the list then?" Frank asked. "It doesn't make sense."

"It could be a smoke screen," Joe said, knowing he was searching for reasons again. "To divert suspicion from Nash."

"That would only work if Rosen and Nash knew they'd be caught," Frank pointed out. "Otherwise, there's no reason to throw us off the track."

Joe had to admit that Frank had a point. "All this is starting to give me a headache," he said finally. "Maybe the theories will come together after we eat."

"A burger certainly wouldn't hurt," Frank said. "And then we can talk to Bo Costello."

"Right," Joe said. They were at the end of the hallway now. Frank pressed the elevator button. "I hope Chet's class is over and he's waiting for us. Now that you've mentioned it, I'm starving."

When they got to the arena, they saw Bo Costello teaching a trapeze class. Joe quickly spotted Chet standing by the seats with the other Bayport High students. Their friend had his neck craned and was watching two trapeze students perform acrobatics. Joe and Frank stood beside Chet.

"It's incredible!" Chet exclaimed, his mouth open. "I'd be scared to death, but they're just flying back and forth as though it were second nature or something. Good thing there's a safety net."

Joe had to agree with his friend. The students

were really skilled. Joe recognized the man who had jumped from the trapeze swing to stand on a platform thirty feet above their heads. "Isn't that Nash up there?" he asked. Chet nodded. Nash's partner swung back and forth on the trapeze as Nash leaned forward on the platform, timing his move.

"Yep," Chet said. "And that's Justine Leone on the trapeze. They're both really good."

"I can tell," Frank said, watching intently.

"You can do the move now, Carl," Joe heard a voice yell up to Nash. He turned to his right to see Bo Costello, his hands around his mouth, hollering up to Nash. "Watch your timing," Costello said. "And don't forget to keep your eyes on Justine."

Joe craned his neck to watch Nash. The student seemed to take Costello's advice to heart. As soon as Justine made her next pass, with her legs hooked around the bar and her arms outstretched, Nash jumped from the platform and went sailing toward her. Joe sucked in his breath as Justine and Carl reached each other. Carl let go of the bar and grabbed Justine's arms.

"All right!" Chet cried out, watching Justine and Carl swing through the air.

"Nice move, Carl," Costello yelled. The students around him clapped politely.

On the next pass, Nash let go of Justine's arms as she grabbed hold of another swing. He then landed back on the platform. Justine swung back to a platform across from Nash, jumping from the trapeze and landing squarely on the platform. She threw the swing toward Nash, who caught it and held it tightly as he stood on the platform.

"Ready when you are, Carl," Costello told his student. "Upside-down swing and reverse twist."

"Huh?" Joe said aloud.

"Circus lingo," Frank said with a wink. "They're famous for it, remember?"

"Right," Joe said, turning back to watch Nash.

The trapeze student grabbed the swing, laced his legs onto it, and let go. As he went sailing from his platform to the one Justine was on, Nash picked up speed. He was flying fast between the two platforms, his arms swinging free. Then, in a flash, Joe saw him unhook his legs from the trapeze.

A few seconds later, Nash had done a midair somersault and was reaching out with his hands for the trapeze swing. The move was solid and sure, and after the somersault, Nash's hands reached familiarly for the swing. He grabbed hold of it and kept swinging, not missing a beat.

"Bravo!" Costello called out.

"Wow," Chet said breathlessly.

Joe couldn't take his eyes off Nash. "The guy's incredible," he said, mesmerized by the sight of Nash swinging back and forth with ease.

All of a sudden, Joe saw the trapeze student

lose his grip. The trapeze started to swing crazily. Nash wrestled with it, fighting to hold on. One end of the swing came unhooked from the chain that supported it. Nash dangled in midair, barely holding on to the wooden rod that until a minute ago had been attached to chains at both ends.

Even from where Joe stood below, he could see the look of horror and fear on Nash's face. Several students around the net gasped in fear.

"Nash!" Joe heard Costello cry out. "Hold on!"

But Joe could tell it was too late. Before his eyes, Carl Nash lost his grip and began to plummet through the air.

"Oh, no!" Costello shouted. "He's going to miss the safety net!"

8 The Airborne Acrobat

Joe saw that Costello was right. Nash was falling so that he was a few inches outside the net. Several students held their hands over their eyes, afraid to look.

Joe stood by, helpless. Then, before his eyes, he saw Nash twist his body around. A second later, he had fallen backward into the net. Nash's acrobat's costume flashed red as he bounced up and down, up and down in the net.

"I can't believe he did that," Joe found himself saying in a hoarse whisper.

"Incredible," Frank said. "That was some trick."

"Truly awesome," Chet said, shaking his head slowly. "I was convinced Carl was a goner."

"I think he's okay," Joe said, pointing toward the net. "See? Bo Costello's with him."

Frank saw Costello help Nash over the net and give him a hand to the ground. Justine had dashed down the ladder from the platform and was standing by them. Costello put his arm around Nash and led him and Justine through the group of students to a nearby seat.

"I'm going to find out what happened to that trapeze," Frank told Chet and his brother. He headed off to the seats where Bo and Nash were sitting.

"We're coming with you," Joe called out.

As Frank got nearer to Nash and Costello, he heard Carl say to his teacher, "I'm telling you the truth. It just fell apart. Right in my hands. Just like that."

Costello's expression was one of shock, and Justine hid her face in her hands. One look at the trio told Frank that this wasn't the time to talk to them—they were much too upset. Instead, he pulled Joe and Chet aside and told them what he had overheard. "Isn't CN the first set of initials on the list?" Frank asked.

"You don't think this was an accident," Joe concluded.

"Not after what Nash just said," Frank replied. "Come on, let's take a look at that trapeze."

He and Joe took off toward the net. Chet

caught up with them at a run. "What do you mean about CN being the first initials on the list?" he asked.

Joe explained to Chet his hunch about the coded message being Rosen's list of accomplices at Circus U. "JL and GU might refer to Justine and Georgianne," Joe finished.

"But Justine was swinging on that trapeze, too," Chet answered. "She could have been the one to fall. Wouldn't Rosen's accomplices pick someone to fall who's *not* listed on that paper?"

"Chet's right," Frank said. "Besides, your theory still has some other holes in it."

"Such as?" Joe asked.

"It doesn't explain what the numbers mean after the initials," Frank said. "And it doesn't explain why Rosen is passing information to his accomplices."

Joe let out a long sigh. "So there are holes. When you two figure out something better, let me know. Until then, I'm following my hunch. Which means that *this* incident was an accident. Let's see if I'm right."

Joe started climbing the ladder that led to the platform where Nash had been standing. When he reached the platform, he stepped off the ladder onto it. The broken trapeze was still hanging from high above the platform. He reached out to grab at the trapeze's dangling bar and heard Chet's voice from below, warning him to be careful.

"We don't want another accident!" he shouted up to Joe.

"Thanks, Chet," Joe muttered to himself. Not daring to look down, he grabbed for the trapeze. He managed to keep his balance as he pulled the trapeze in close. He examined the broken end of the wooden bar. The metal hook that the rope was tied to was broken. Someone had obviously bent the metal several times, weakening it until it could break easily.

"So much for my theory," Joe said as he untied the other end of the wooden rod from the rope. He stuck it in his back pocket and made his way down the ladder.

"What did you find?" Frank asked when his brother was on the floor again. When Joe showed him the rod, Frank nodded in understanding. "It looks like Circus U.'s been struck again," he agreed.

"And it looks like the people on the list are victims, not accomplices," Joe added. "Unless Nash *is* Rosen's accomplice, and his plan to make Justine fall backfired."

"But then why are Nash's initials on the list?" Frank asked.

"And Georgianne, too," Joe said. He looked over at where Justine and Nash had been sitting with Costello, but the three of them were gone. Apparently Costello had dismissed the class, because the other students were walking toward the backstage area.

"We should tell Dean Turner about this incident," Frank said.

"That's a good idea, except that Dean Turner had an appointment, remember?" Joe pointed out.

"True," Frank said, running his hands through his hair. "What's our plan, then?"

Joe thought for a moment. "We can still follow up on Ralph Rosen. Dean Turner told us that Bo Costello could give us some information about him. I still think he's an important link in the accidents here," he insisted.

"We don't know that for sure, but I agree we should talk to Costello," Frank said.

"What about lunch?" Chet asked.

"As soon as we talk to Bo," Joe said with a laugh, "we'll grab a burger."

"Okay," Chet said grudgingly.

Joe led the way down to Costello's office. When they got there, they knocked on the door. There was no answer. Joe opened the door a crack. He saw that Costello was on the phone, and heard him tell the person on the other end to "take it easy and be careful."

Bo spotted Joe, Frank, and Chet, and quickly said goodbye into the phone.

"Come on in!" Bo called heartily. "You guys are the Bayport High students, right?"

Joe nodded, guessing that Turner had told

Costello that he and Frank were in training along with Chet.

"I was just talking to a former student," Costello told them when they were inside his office. "I like to stay in touch with my students. See how they're doing, you know."

Joe saw his brother smile. "They must like hearing from you, too," Frank said.

Bo laughed. "Oh, they do. Sometimes they even stop by when we're on tour, if they're in the area."

Joe ran his eyes around the room, surprised at how much stuff Bo had crammed into the tiny space. All along one wall was a huge bulletin board covered with maps, photographs of what looked like Bo in his circus days, head shots of former Circus U. students, and all kinds of schedules and dates of the winter tour.

"Those are lists of all the major circuses across the United States," Costello explained, following Joe's gaze. "Their schedules, their personnel, everything. Even though we're on tour, we still have to run Circus U."

"Is that how you keep track of your students?" Chet asked, pointing to the bulletin board.

"Yep," Bo said, nodding. "It's all there. If I see that one of them is heading toward us in Florida or when we're on tour, I'll try to track him or her down, tell the kid to stop by and say hello."

"That's really nice," Joe said. "I bet they appreciate your interest."

"Oh, they do." Bo paused and gave Joe a curious look. "Is there something I can help you with?" he asked.

Joe turned his eyes from the bulletin board. "Yes, there is," he said, realizing he had to be careful about what he said. Because he and Frank were undercover, it wasn't a good idea to tell Costello the whole truth.

"Last night a juggler with the Montero Brothers Circus named Ralph Rosen dropped a ball in Chet's tote bag," Joe explained. "Inside the ball was a message. And, well, we were thinking that maybe, just maybe, the message has something to do with the accidents here at the circus. We thought you should know because the people listed in the message are connected to Circus U."

"We also thought you might be able to tell us if Ralph Rosen is the kind of guy who might try to cause these accidents," Frank said. "Dean Turner mentioned that he had been kicked out of Circus U. We think he might be trying to get back at people there."

Costello sat down on the edge of his desk. He was silent for a moment. "I'm shocked," he said finally. "I knew Ralph Rosen had problems, but I would never have suspected that he would stoop so low." Costello shook his head sadly. "I'm also

79

appalled to think that a former Circus U. student would do such a terrible thing."

Costello paused for a moment, then gave the Hardys and Chet a curious look. "Why are you all interested in figuring out why we've been having these accidents, anyway?"

Joe glanced at Frank and saw his brother's warning look. He turned back to Costello.

"As students here, we're anxious about the accidents that have already happened," Joe said carefully. "First the cannon misfired and Dean Turner nearly suffocated. And then, when we saw what happened to Carl Nash on the trapeze just now, we started thinking. Since you're director of admissions, we figured if anyone would know about Ralph Rosen, it would be you," he finished.

Costello let out a hearty laugh. "Doing a bit of amateur detecting, eh? Well, while you boys are at Circus U., why don't you stick to clowning and learning about other kinds of circus performing. Don't worry. We'll manage to settle our problems."

"Do you have some background info on Rosen in your files?" Joe pressed.

Costello stood up from the edge of his desk and shook his head slowly. "I might, but that information is confidential. Only Dean Turner can release it. Come on, guys," he said finally. "I really appreciate what you're trying to do, but why don't you leave all this stuff to the people in charge? Kick back, relax, and enjoy your classes here. You won't get another chance like this in—"

Before Costello could finish his sentence, his phone began to ring. "Excuse me," he said to the three of them.

Joe stood up and headed for the door, realizing they weren't going to get anywhere with the dean of admissions. Frank and Chet followed. "We'll let you get back to work," Frank said.

"Thanks," Costello said, picking up the phone on the third ring. "Take my advice: Enjoy yourselves and don't worry, okay?"

"That was a big waste of time," Joe said when the three of them were back in the hall. "We didn't even get a look at Rosen's application."

"We'll just have to find out about Rosen another way," Frank said, trying to reassure his brother. "We can ask Jim Jacobs where he's staying."

"Uh, do you guys mind if we get some lunch first?" Chet said. "I don't think I can go on much longer without some fuel inside me."

Joe laughed. "Okay, Chet. Frank and I know that clowning around is hungry work."

"So is detecting," Frank said. "Let's head over to that new burger place on Main Street."

"Great," Chet said. "I hear they have foot-high burgers."

"They must have thought of you when they came up with their menu," Joe said with a grin.

With Joe in the lead, they walked past the elevators, then down the hall toward the exit that led to the parking lot. When they reached the exit, Joe turned to say something to Frank and Chet. Suddenly, a figure at the end of the hall by the elevators caught his eye—a figure wearing green striped baggy pants dotted with rhine-stones and an unmistakable blue wig.

"Hey, Frank," Joe said slowly, his excitement building.

"What?" Frank asked, facing Joe.

Joe pointed down the long hall to where the juggler was still standing, his back to them, waiting for an elevator.

"Don't look now," he said, "but I think we just found Ralph Rosen."

9 Ralph Rosen Returns

"Hey!" Frank called out. "Hey, you!"

The young man turned around to see who was shouting at him. Despite the fact that the juggler wasn't wearing clown makeup, Frank was sure it was Rosen. The costume was the same as the one he'd seen the previous night. As soon as Rosen saw Frank, he turned to the left and ran down the hall.

"He knows exactly who we are!" Frank shouted to Joe. "Let's get him," he said, taking off at a clip.

He saw Rosen turn into a stairwell that led up to the backstage area and the arena. Frank ran up the stairs after him, keeping an eye on Rosen's fleeting green pants. Joe and Chet were close

83

behind. Soon they were chasing Rosen through the crowded arena, and people were flying out of the way on either side of them.

"Stop that clown!" Frank shouted to a woman who was just about to walk in front of Rosen. "Don't let him get away!"

The woman heard Frank, but too late. Rosen pushed her aside, and she went flying to the floor. As Frank ran past her, he slowed down briefly to make sure she was okay and then picked up speed again as Rosen darted through the red velvet curtain into the arena.

Frank pushed the curtain aside and came to a quick stop, searching for Rosen's green striped pants. Rosen was nowhere in sight. Instead, Frank was greeted by the sight of two animal cages. Inside the cages were a lion and a tiger. Then Frank spotted something else—a trapdoor in the center ring that had been left open.

"So that's where he went," Frank said aloud. "Down the trapdoor the clowns use to fool the audience into thinking tons of people are getting out of a little car." The nearby tiger let out a low growl, making Frank jump.

"I'm outta here," Frank said under his breath. Where were Joe and Chet? he wondered.

He was about to turn back to look for them when a voice at Frank's side said sharply, "You bet you're out of here!" Frank felt someone grab his arm and steer him around.

"Hey! What do you—" Frank began.

The woman who had a hold on his elbow was dressed in a security guard uniform. She had the greenest eyes Frank had ever seen. At her side were Chet and Joe, looking glum.

"This area is off limits," the woman went on, tightening her grip on Frank's arm. "I don't know who you kids are, but you obviously don't belong here."

Frank felt himself turn red, then he breathlessly tried to explain. "We're students at Circus U. We were just going to try out that trapdoor the clowns use."

"Yeah, right," the woman said, glaring at Frank, Joe, and Chet. "And I'm the Queen of England."

"We really are students," Joe insisted.

"I saw you chasing that guy," the woman said. "You nearly hurt someone back there. I don't know what you're doing here, but you'd better leave before I call security."

"I'm trying to tell you," Frank said. "We're students."

From the look on the woman's face, Frank could tell he wasn't getting anywhere. He pulled himself out of her grip and stood by Joe with his arms folded. The tiger in the cage across from them sank down onto the floor, crossing his paws under him and giving them all a wary look.

"I have a student pass," Chet said, digging into

his pocket and pulling out a card. He showed the card to the woman. "My friends here are brand-new students and they don't have passes yet."

The woman looked at Chet's pass and nodded. "Okay, but you three are still not allowed in the arena without a Circus U. instructor. This area," she continued, gesturing toward the animal cages, "is very dangerous right now. The animals are about to rehearse with their trainers, and only professional circus people are allowed here."

Frank realized it was useless to try to convince her to let them stay. He sighed, looked toward the trapdoor, and knew they'd have to go after Rosen some other way. "Right," he said, turning away. "Come on, guys. Let's get out of here."

"Thanks, Chet," Joe said as they walked away. "You probably saved us from being kicked out of the building for good."

"No problem," Chet said. "But you guys had better get yourselves a couple of passes."

Frank nodded. "Up till now, we've been lucky. We've either been able to sneak past security guards or no one's noticed us."

"What are we going to do now that we've lost Rosen again?" Joe asked his brother as they left the arena through the front exit and began to round the building toward the parking lot.

Frank stopped for a moment and rubbed his chin. "We know Rosen's still around the circus. When Dean Turner gets back, he can get us those passes. Maybe we can get him to write out special passes that will allow us to go everywhere in the building."

"We can also ask the dean to get us access to Rosen's file. Let's stop by his office before we leave for lunch to find out when he'll be back."

The three boys made a quick detour back into the building to Dean Turner's office. The dean's secretary, who was using the office next door, informed them that Turner wouldn't be back that afternoon—he was running late and he had to meet another donor out of the office later that afternoon.

"Rats," Frank said as they headed down the hall toward the exit. "Where does that leave us?" he asked.

"Hungry, for one," Chet said, holding his stomach. "The pangs—they're too much," he added dramatically, bending over.

"What's that?" Joe asked his friend. "Rehearsal for when you play the tragic clown?"

"Give me a break!" Chet cried, heading off down the hall. "Detecting is hungry work. You said so yourself before we ran off chasing Ralph Rosen."

Joe shrugged, looked at Frank, and followed Chet out the door. "He's right, you know. Even detectives have to eat."

Frank stopped for a moment and tried to think of a way through the dead end they were in.

Turner was out, Bo Costello wouldn't help, Georgianne Unger . . .

"Hey," he called out to Joe and Chet. "You guys, hold it."

Joe turned around. "What's up?" he asked.

Frank jogged up to where Joe was standing. "We haven't questioned Georgianne Unger yet. After all, she's a prime suspect. Maybe she's the one helping Rosen out."

Frank watched his brother think for a moment, then shake his head slowly. "No good. She's not going to give anything away if she's involved in the sabotage."

"I guess you're right," Frank admitted. "We'll just have to get those passes from Dean Turner and do some more searching. It kills me to waste so much time, though."

"Come on," Joe urged. "We'll grab a bite and have another look at the message. Maybe we can make some headway there."

Frank gave in and followed Joe. In a few minutes, they were all back in the van on their way to the burger place in downtown Bayport. After downing two burgers apiece and some extra-large fries, Frank and Joe dropped Chet off at home. His classes were done for the day, and he was going back to Circus U. that night for the performance of the Montero Brothers Circus.

"You guys are going to come tonight, aren't

you?" Chet asked as he hopped out of the van. "It should be a fantastic show."

Frank nodded. "It'll be a good chance to see Turner and do some more investigating," he said.

"I'm glad I didn't go for the foot-high burger at lunch," Chet said with a grin. "Now I'll have more room for some great circus food tonight. Peanuts, popcorn, cotton candy, franks, sodas . . ."

"Uh, we'll pick you up in two hours," Joe interrupted, rolling his eyes.

"Great," Chet said. "That gives me time to practice what I learned today."

"You're not going to the performance in clown makeup, are you?" Joe asked. "You wouldn't embarrass us like that, would you?"

Chet let out a huge laugh. "Just you wait and see," he said, racing up the sidewalk to his front door.

Frank was quiet as he drove the rest of the way home. By the time he parked the van in the driveway, Joe had rattled off all the facts of the case, but Frank had hardly paid attention. He kept thinking that there was something he should be remembering about what he had seen—a connection he should be making.

"Oh, well," he said absently, unlocking the front door. "I guess it will come to me."

"What will?" Joe wanted to know. He looked

at his brother. "Have you been listening to a word I've been saying the whole way home?"

"Not really," Frank admitted as they headed upstairs. "I think I'll lie down for a while before we have to pick up Chet."

"Me, too," Joe said, opening the door to his room.

From the hall, Frank heard his brother let out a loud yell.

"What is it?" Frank cried, rushing to the door of Joe's room.

Inside, he saw what had made Joe yell. The room was a shambles. Papers were strewn all over. The window was broken and glass was everywhere.

Then Frank looked down and gasped. His brother lay facedown on the floor in the middle of the room. A masked man in a black, hooded jumpsuit held Joe's arms behind his back. The man had Ralph Rosen's gem-studded juggler's ball in his hand and was about to knock Joe out cold with it!

10 Trapeze Thief

Before Frank could react, the masked man let go of Joe and rushed to the window. Rosen's ball was in his left hand, and his right hand reached out the window for a piece of rope that was hanging by the frame.

"We've got to stop him," Joe called to his brother. Joe hurried to the window, but the masked man had already sailed through it, airborne, the rope carrying him to a tree ten feet away.

Joe leaned out the window, careful to avoid broken glass, and felt a blast of cold air. "He's climbing down the tree!" he cried. "He's getting away!"

"Not if I can help it," Frank said, running from

the room. Joe followed him down the stairs, out the door, and into the cold. They rushed around to the side of the house and spotted the masked man running across the backyard.

Frank and Joe picked up their pace, determined not to let the man get away. They chased him through the backyard and through the neighbor's. Soon, they were on a street, and Joe saw the man running for a car.

"He's getting away!" Joe cried out to Frank.

Joe dashed across the street to where the masked man was getting into a blue sports car with Texas plates. Joe caught up with him just as the man had closed his door. The man started the car and put it into gear. Joe saw Rosen's ball lying on the seat next to him. It was their only lead— and it had been stolen right out from under them.

With a squeal of tires, the car turned sharply to the left, knocking Joe down. Then it sped off down the street.

Frank rushed over to where Joe lay on the pavement. "Are you okay?" he asked his brother, giving him a hand up.

Joe got up and dusted off his jeans. "I'm fine. I just wish that guy hadn't gotten away."

"Me, too," Frank said, following the speeding car with his eyes. "Come on," he urged. "Let's go back home and see what the damage is."

Back inside his room, Joe surveyed the scene. The ball was gone. His papers were all over the floor. The room was getting cold from the broken window. Joe went over to the window and looked at the rope that hung from the nearby tree.

"Whoever this robber was, he sure was pretty agile," Joe said as Frank stepped into the room with a dustpan and broom.

"Like someone in the circus," Frank offered.

"A trapeze artist, say?" Joe asked, suddenly thinking of Carl Nash's accident early that day.

"Exactly," Frank said. He started sweeping up the broken glass and putting it in a trash can. "The car had Texas plates. Didn't Carl Nash say he was from Texas?"

"That's right," Joe said. He began to pick up the papers on the floor. "What if Rosen and Nash are accomplices?"

"It's an idea," Frank admitted. "Except that we don't know why Rosen would have been passing that ball to Nash, or what Nash is helping Rosen do."

"Sabotage," Joe said, frustrated. "I've been trying to tell you that Rosen wants to foul things up at Circus U. because he got kicked out."

"Look, Joe," Frank said. "You keep assuming that Rosen's message has to do with the accidents, but according to Paul Turner, these accidents started in Florida six months ago. Where was Rosen all that time? And the Montero has only been on tour for a few weeks."

Joe had to admit his brother had a point. He

picked up the trash can, gave the broken window one last look, and sat down at his desk. "What if Rosen's been passing instructions to Nash in the balls all this time?" Joe asked finally. "What if this is just one in a series of messages?"

Frank shook his head slowly. "You really want to make your theory about the coded message work, don't you?" he said with a smile. "Assuming Rosen was hanging around Circus U., it still doesn't make sense that he would take the trouble to pass messages in a juggler's ball. Why not make a phone call? Why not meet Nash in secret?"

"I don't know," Joe said with a sigh, holding his head in his hands.

"And why would Nash's initials be on the list anyway, if he were Rosen's accomplice?" Frank continued.

"All right already," Joe said in an exasperated tone. "I give up. I can't answer any of those questions, and I'm even willing to admit my theory has some holes in it, but we're not getting anywhere on this mystery."

Frank sat down on the bed across from Joe. "I think we need to get back to the facts," he explained. "See what we can piece together from what we know."

"Instead of pulling things out of thin air, you mean," Joe said, lifting his head up. "Okay," he said grudgingly. "What are the facts?"

Frank counted off on his fingers. "One. It looks like Rosen meant to pass his ball to Carl Nash, and that Nash probably—"

"Oh, no, you don't," Joe interrupted. "No probablys. Just the facts."

"That someone who happens to be an acrobat broke in here and stole Rosen's ball," Frank finished.

"We also know that there are people at Circus U. who would benefit if Paul Turner lost his job because of these accidents," Joe offered.

"Georgianne Unger, for one," Frank said. "Even though Turner thinks she'd never get the job."

"And Bo Costello," Joe added. "Remember what Turner said about Bo being one of the people with the experience to do his job."

"Right," Frank said. "We shouldn't rule out Costello as a suspect."

"None of this explains how Rosen is related to the accidents, though," Joe said.

Frank pulled a slip of paper out of his shirt pocket. Joe leaned over and saw it was the coded message. "It's in here, somewhere," Frank said. "The clue to Rosen's connection has got to be in this message."

"Too bad we can't decode it," Joe said glumly. "But let's have another go at it, anyway."

He pulled his chair closer to the bed, and Frank unfolded the paper. Joe scratched his head, looking at the series of initials and numbers for what felt like the thousandth time: CN/1220; JL/103; GU/214.

For the next hour, Joe and Frank played with combinations, rearranging the letters, connecting them to different numbers, adding and subtracting the numbers, and rearranging the letters yet again. "What if these numbers are actually dates?" Joe finally suggested. "I mean, it's a long shot, but it's possible."

Frank looked over Joe's shoulder as Joe wrote them out. "See—twelve-twenty. That could be December twentieth, right?"

Frank nodded, and Joe went on. "And one-oh-three. That might mean January third."

"And two-fourteen could be February fourteenth," Frank said.

"Exactly." Joe checked his watch. He remembered they'd told Chet they would pick him up at six, and it was already ten till. Then the date on his watch caught his attention. It was December nineteenth—one day before the first date on the list.

"Hey, Frank," Joe said, slowly turning to his brother with a huge grin on his face. "Guess what day it is."

Frank leaned back in his chair. "I don't have to guess. It's the nineteenth. Hey—wait a minute. If we're right about this message, that means something is going to happen tomorrow."

96

"You guessed it," Joe said. "If we're right, it also means that the code has nothing to do with the sabotage," he admitted ruefully, "since Nash's accident happened today, not tomorrow."

Frank shrugged and smiled. "There goes your theory. Sorry about that."

Joe chose to ignore his brother's comment. Instead, he grabbed his jacket. "We've got to pick up Chet. And since we know that according to Rosen's code nothing more is going to happen until tomorrow, I'm going to enjoy myself tonight. No mysteries, no theories, no false leads."

"Just good honest fun, right?" Frank asked.

"Right," Joe said firmly.

"I still think we should try to track down Rosen," Frank said. "The sooner we find out what he's up to, the better. Besides, *someone* is sabotaging the circus. We need to find out who it is and stop him or her."

"Come on, Frank. One night's not going to make a difference," Joe said. "We need some R and R."

Frank seemed reluctant to give up on the investigation just yet. "I don't know if taking the night off is such a good idea," he said.

"We probably won't be able to get backstage, anyway," Joe reminded him. "Circus U. isn't in session, and there's no reception tonight. You should learn how to chill out."

From the smile on Frank's face, Joe could see

he was starting to get through to his brother. "Okay?" he asked.

"Okay," Frank said finally.

"Good. Let's go."

The next morning, Joe talked with Chet the whole way to the Bayport Arena about the circus performance the night before. "I can't decide who was the best," Frank said. "That guy doing back flips on the high wire, the bareback riders doing handstands on their horses, or the clowns."

"The clowns were really a riot," Joe agreed. "I can definitely see Chet up there spraying seltzer on the mayor of Bayport."

"The mayor looked like he loved it," Frank said.

"You should think about giving up detective work to become a professional circus performer, Joe," Chet said.

"No way, Chet," Frank said as he parked the van. "I need Joe in *my* act."

Chet laughed as he jumped out of the van. "Think about it, Joe," he said. "I've got to run. I have a juggling class."

"Sorry, but we have to cut class again," Joe said, zipping up his jacket against the cold. "We're going to take private lessons from our mystery juggler—Ralph Rosen."

Chet laughed, and his breath billowed out in white gusts. "Good luck, you guys."

"Thanks," Frank said, watching Chet run off toward the back entrance to the arena. Joe and Frank headed in the same direction. When they stepped into the building, Joe said, "Maybe we should find Dean Turner and have him get us clearance. I don't want to run into that security guard again."

"I don't see any guards this morning," Frank said, opening the door slowly and looking around. "It looks like we won't need passes. I guess the guards don't go on duty until later."

They headed down the hall, glancing to the left and right to see if Rosen was in any of the rooms they were passing.

"I hope Rosen is here," Joe said. "I'm ready to have a nice long chat with him about what scheme he planned for today."

"If Jim Jacobs is around, he can tell us where Rosen is," Frank said.

"It doesn't look like anyone's around," Joe said, glancing up and down the hallway. "This hallway's pretty deserted."

Soon they were at the room the clowns called clown alley. Joe didn't spot Jim Jacobs, so he asked a woman if she knew where they could find Ralph Rosen. She pointed to a small room down the hall.

"For some reason, he rates his own dressing room," the woman said, shaking her head as she walked away.

When they reached the room, Frank went up close to it, held his finger to his lips, and motioned for Joe to be quiet. Joe stood back from his brother. He looked up at the transom window over the door and saw that there was a light on in the room. "He must be here," he called out to Frank in an excited whisper.

Frank nodded and took a few steps back. He stood on tiptoe, trying to see over the transom.

"If he's in, we'll just confront him with what we know, make him give us some explanations," Joe said. "If not, we'll just let ourselves in and wait."

Joe waited for Frank to answer. When he didn't, Joe glanced over his shoulder. "Frank?" he asked. "What do you think?"

Then he turned and saw why his brother hadn't answered right away. He had been knocked out and was lying faceup on the floor with an ugly red mark on his forehead.

Joe rushed over and knelt down beside his brother. "Frank!" he cried.

Then Joe sensed that someone had come up behind him. Suddenly he felt a whopping blow to his head. Joe sank to the floor, unconscious.

11 Clowns
Undercover

Frank Hardy felt himself coming to, and thought that his head felt as if someone had stored it in a freezer overnight. When he tried to move there was a cold, dull throbbing at his temples that could only mean one thing: he'd been knocked out.

Frank opened his eyes. He slowly realized that his hands and legs were tied to the chair he was sitting in. He glanced around and noted that he was inside a small room that looked to be about the same size as Rosen's.

"Ralph Rosen," Frank mumbled to himself, trying to move as slowly as possible until he was fully awake. "It must have been him."

"Mmmm," Frank heard Joe murmur. Frank

turned as much as he could with his hands tied together behind his back and saw Joe lying on the floor next to him. His brother was tied up, too.

When Joe opened his eyes, he looked up and saw Frank looking at him. "Where are we?" Joe mumbled, trying to pull himself up to a sitting position. The effort was obviously too much, because Joe quickly eased himself back down to the ground. "My head's killing me."

"Mine, too," Frank said, stretching his neck to get his circulation going again. "Rosen really did a number on us."

"Rosen!" Joe cried. "That guy's going to be in big trouble when I finally meet up with him."

"Let's concentrate on getting out of here," Frank said. "Do you think you could move over to the door and see if it's locked?"

"I'll try," Joe said. He eased himself up in a sitting position. "Ouch," he said, wincing in pain. "I don't think I'm ready to move yet."

Frank scanned the room, looking for some kind of sharp object to cut the ropes that bound them.

"Rosen was crazy to do this to us," Joe said. "This makes him look more guilty than ever."

Frank didn't answer. He was still looking around the room for a knife or scissors.

"He's gone to a lot of trouble to put us out of commission," Joe said. "It's almost like he wanted us out of the way, but only until he had time to come back and figure out what to do with us."

Frank spotted a bag leaning against the far wall of the room. "Do you think you could get to that bag?" he asked his brother, pointing to it with his head. "There might be something in the bag we can use to cut these ropes."

Joe pulled himself up and edged over to the side of the room. He grabbed the bag's handle between his teeth and carried it over to Frank.

Frank leaned over as best he could to look inside the bag. He spotted more of Rosen's juggling balls and some bowling pins—and then, underneath a clown wig, Frank saw a knife handle.

"There," he said, pointing it out to Joe. "Look. There's a knife in the bag."

Joe turned around, grabbed the bag with his fingers, and shook it until Rosen's props spilled out. A knife fell from the bag on top of the pile.

Joe turned around and faced the pile of props. "It's a stage knife," he said.

Frank saw the plastic handle and realized his brother was right. "It might still work," Frank urged. "Grab it and see if it's sharp enough."

Joe twisted sideways and used his hand to pick up the knife. He turned with his back to Frank and tried working the knots. "Forget it," he said finally. "There's no way this thing is going to cut through the rope."

Frank gritted his teeth, sensing that they were wasting precious time. Whatever Rosen had planned, he stood a much better chance of succeeding with him and Joe tied up like this.

"Wait a minute!" Joe cried, twisting around and facing Frank.

"What?" Frank asked.

"I just thought of something." Joe pulled himself to his feet and hopped over to Rosen's makeup table. "Yes!" he cried.

"What?" Frank felt himself getting frustrated. "Would you please tell me what it is that you thought of?" He twisted his head. Out of the corner of his eye, he saw that Joe had his back to Rosen's table. In one quick move, Joe had picked something up from the table, let it drop to the ground, and stepped on it with his shoe.

"Perfect!" Joe cried, looking at the floor.

Frank followed Joe's gaze and saw a small hand mirror, shattered into several pieces, lying on the floor. "Good job," Frank said. "But be careful."

Joe nodded and eased himself down to the floor again. In a few seconds he'd managed to pick up a shard of the mirror and was edging his way back to Frank. "Don't move," he urged his brother.

Frank waited silently, holding his breath, while he felt Joe work at the rope holding his hands together. "Almost there," Joe said with encouragement. "Got it."

"Way to go!" Frank shouted. He pulled his hands apart and felt the rope drop to the ground. He rubbed his wrists to get the circulation going again, and then leaned over to untie his legs. "You're next," he told Joe.

Joe turned his back to Frank, and within a few minutes Frank had untied his brother's hands. Joe took care of the rope around his ankles himself. "Now what?" he asked Frank.

"If we're going to find Rosen, we'll need a cover." Frank got up and started searching the room. "If we're in disguise, he won't know we're after him."

"And he won't have a chance to get away," Joe added.

Frank stopped short for a moment and turned to face Joe. "Hey, what did you say earlier about Rosen not being involved in the sabotage?"

Joe looked embarrassed, then confessed, "It doesn't make sense anymore. Why would he go so far to get us out of commission?"

Frank bit his lower lip, thinking. "He wouldn't. Not unless there was something specific he was up to—something he had to do today and he thought we might be in the way."

"Because today's December twentieth," Joe said.

"Exactly," Frank replied. "And as we said before, Nash's accident happened yesterday. Rosen could still be behind the sabotage, but the message must mean something different. We don't have time right now to figure out what it is, though." He continued hunting around the trailer for a disguise. "I think I found it!" he said in a minute. "Look."

Frank pulled a red and white polka-dotted clown costume out of Rosen's trunk. Under that costume was another one, with orange and black polka dots. Also in the trunk were two pairs of long shoes with flowers standing up at the tips and two more wigs. "These are perfect. I've seen clowns wearing costumes that look exactly like these. Rosen will never know these are his costumes." Frank held out the red and white costume to his brother.

Joe took one look and shook his head. "No way are you getting me in that thing."

"It's the only way," Frank said, putting his leg into the costume. "Hurry up. We can't let Rosen get away."

Joe took the costume from Frank and looked at it. "This is ridiculous," he said.

Frank passed Joe a wig from the trunk. "Are you going to put the suit on or not?" he asked.

Joe must have realized that Frank meant business, because he quickly stuck his legs in the costume and pulled it on. "I'm not wearing that wig, though."

"It's no disguise if you don't put on the wig," Frank told him. "Come on, already."

Joe stuck the wig on his head. "Satisfied?" he asked.

Frank looked at Joe and burst out laughing. The polka-dotted costume made Joe look huge, and the red wig gave his face a boyish look. "You look like a real clown," he said, stifling his laughter. He reached for the clown make-up on Rosen's table. "But we'll need whiteface, too."

Joe shook his head vigorously. "No way," he insisted.

Frank reached into a jar of white makeup and started smearing it on his face. "Without make-up, our costumes aren't very authentic."

Joe sighed and started applying the makeup. "It's too bad we missed Chet's makeup class. If we'd gone, we'd know what we're doing right now."

"Improvise," Frank urged, reaching for a large tube of red lipstick and applying it to his mouth. He drew a circle above his lips and around his mouth and filled it in with lipstick. "And hurry. We don't have much time."

In a few minutes, Frank and Joe were completely in costume, clown face, wigs, and shoes. "Let's go!" Frank urged when he saw Joe was done drawing thick eyebrows and smearing his eyelids with black makeup.

Frank eased the door to Rosen's dressing room open, peeked into the hallway, and saw that it was empty. He stepped out of the room and motioned for Joe to follow him.

"Just act casual," Frank urged his brother under his breath. "If we prowl around long enough, we're sure to spot Rosen."

"It's kind of hard to act casual when you're dressed like a dork," Joe told his brother.

Frank ignored the comment and strolled down the hallway, his huge shoes flapping in front of him. Around them, the Montero Brothers Circus was getting ready for that afternoon's performance. Clowns and other performers moved back and forth between dressing rooms and prop rooms, and prop people carried stilts and toy cars toward the freight elevator.

"He's got to be around here somewhere," Frank told Joe.

"Unless he took off once and for all," Joe told him.

"But it's the twentieth," Frank reminded his brother. "According to his code, something's going to happen today."

As soon as the words were out of his mouth, Frank spotted Rosen's telltale baggy green striped pants coming out of clown alley.

"There he is," Frank whispered, trying not to be heard. "Come on!"

Frank took off at a brisk walk, trying not to arouse Rosen's suspicion. Joe followed in step.

"Easy, now," Frank warned his brother. "Don't catch up to him too quickly."

"Don't worry," Joe muttered, reaching up to straighten his wig. "At the rate I'm going, I won't be able to catch up with *you!*"

As they got closer, Frank felt his heart beating triple-time. They were about to nab the mysterious juggler once and for all.

Rosen turned around and looked toward them. Frank held his breath. He hoped Rosen wouldn't recognize them.

The juggler did a double take, looking puzzled. Then he turned back to the woman he was talking to and handed her something. Frank was still too far away to see what it was.

"We've got to get him," Joe hissed under his breath. "I'm not letting that guy get away again."

"Keep cool," Frank urged, watching Rosen talk to the woman. The Hardys moved a bit closer and heard Rosen say, "Get out of here." Then he turned so that his back was to Frank and Joe.

Joe grabbed his brother's arm. "What's he doing?" he asked.

"I don't know," Frank said under his breath. Then, before Frank could say another word, Rosen took off at a brisk pace down the hall.

"Get him!" Frank cried out.

Joe surged ahead, with Frank not far behind. Rosen was still a good twenty feet away. He looked over his shoulder at the Hardys and broke into a run.

Frank and Joe came up quickly on the short, blond woman who had been talking to Rosen. What they saw shocked them—and stopped them both dead in their tracks.

The woman was Justine Leone. And in her hands was one of Rosen's gem-studded balls!

12 The Plot Thickens

"Justine!" Joe and Frank cried in unison.

The girl stared at them, a look of confusion in her blue eyes. "Do I know you guys?" she asked.

To his left, Joe saw Rosen disappear into an elevator. "Go after him, Frank," he urged his brother. "I'll stay here and find out what this is all about."

"Right," Frank shouted. "Good luck!"

Joe turned back to face Justine, realizing the girl didn't recognize him in his costume. "It's Joe Hardy. I'm Chet Morton's friend. And a part-time student at Circus U.," he added hastily.

Justine leaned in to get a better look at Joe. "Oh, right," she said with a shrug. "I've seen you guys around. What are you doing dressed up like a clown?" she asked.

"I don't really have time to explain," Joe said. "What's more important is how well you know that guy who was just here."

Justine frowned. "Which guy?" she asked in a defensive tone.

"The one who gave you this," Joe said, taking the green, gem-studded ball from her hands.

"I never met him before in my life," Justine said, tossing back her long blond hair.

"So how did he know you well enough to hand this ball over to you?" Joe demanded, holding it up for her to see.

The trapeze student stood there, her arms crossed over her red, white, and blue Circus U. warm-up suit. She bit her lower lip as she thought about what to say. Finally she spoke up. "I don't know."

"That's no answer," Joe said. "He talked to you. He told you to get out of here. He must have known you pretty well to say that."

"I don't know what the fuss is all about," Justine insisted. "I was just doing a friend a favor, that's all."

Joe was about to ask Justine who her friend was when Frank came running back. "He got away," Frank said breathlessly. He wiped the sweat off his face with the sleeve of his clown costume and smudged the makeup. "I got to the parking lot and saw someone tearing out of here in one of the Montero vans. I didn't get a good look at the driver, but I'll bet you anything it was Rosen."

Joe nodded grimly. Rosen had gotten away yet again. "Justine says she was doing a friend a favor by taking the ball from Rosen."

Frank shot the trapeze student a suspicious look. "Oh, really?" he asked. "And who's your friend?"

Justine swallowed a few times and reached for the ball in Joe's hands. "I don't have time to stand around here gabbing."

Joe held the ball out of her reach. "Not so fast," he said. "You have a few questions to answer first."

"Look," Justine said, her voice rising in anger, "I don't have to answer any of your questions. I told you I was doing a favor for a friend. I really don't know what your problem is."

"I think you're the one with the problem," Joe began in an angry voice.

Frank put a hand on Joe's arm. "Go easy, Joe," he said.

"Why should I?" Joe asked, turning to his brother. "Her initials are on Rosen's list, too. She's in on it, Frank. She's got to be."

"In on what?" Justine asked. "What do you mean about my initials being on some list?"

Frank leaned toward Joe and whispered in his ear, "We still don't know what that list means, brother," he warned. "Don't blow it. If she's involved somehow, you're not going to get anywhere by threatening her."

Justine watched them with a wide-eyed look. "Would you mind telling me what's going on here?"

Joe took a deep breath and smiled at Justine. "Um, actually," he said, "we don't really know what's going on here, to tell you the truth. So why don't you tell us who your friend is?"

Justine rolled her eyes. "You guys are too much. Okay. Carl asked me to meet this guy here. He said the guy had something for him, but Carl couldn't meet him. He had something to do for Bo Costello. I told him I'd do it."

Frank raised an eyebrow at Joe.

"Carl Nash," Joe said.

"Our acrobatic friend strikes again," Frank said.

"What are you talking about?" Justine asked, her eyes moving back and forth between Frank and Joe.

Joe ignored her question and asked, "Did the guy who gave you this know who you were?"

Justine shrugged. "He seemed to. I mean, he didn't ask me my name or anything. I guess Carl told him I'd be here."

"Something's not right here," Frank said, shaking his head. "If this ball is so important, why didn't Nash come for it himself?"

"You'll have to ask him," Justine retorted, stamping the ground with her foot. "But you'd better give the ball back to me," she insisted, holding her hand out. "I'm supposed to meet Carl in ten minutes in the animal room."

"Let's go find Nash," Frank said to his brother. "We can ask him ourselves what's going on."

"I know one thing," Joe said. "He's in this up to his neck."

While Joe's attention was on his brother, Justine grabbed the ball from his hands. "That's mine," she said, pulling her hands away when Joe reached to get it back. With that, she headed off at a brisk walk in the direction of the animal room.

Joe followed a distance behind with Frank beside him. "We can't let Nash get that ball," Joe said. "There's probably another message inside."

Frank reached up to scratch under his wig. "We're going to have to nab Nash before he can get his hands on it."

Joe kept his eyes on Justine in front of them. They were walking toward the animal room. He wanted to make sure Justine didn't pass the ball to Nash before he and Frank could stop her.

"I think Justine knows we're following her," Frank whispered to Joe. "Maybe I'm wrong and she's not involved in whatever's going on between Nash and Rosen. Maybe she's not worried we're following her because she has nothing to hide."

"But then why did Rosen pick her to pass the ball to Nash?" Joe whispered back.

"I don't know," Frank admitted, as he steered clear of an animal trainer leading a seal on a leash. The smell of animals was overpowering now. The Hardys saw Justine enter the huge room.

"Nash trusts her," Frank said. "Maybe that's enough explanation. Nash must have told Rosen to expect Justine. Why else would the guy have passed the ball to her?"

They looked into the room and saw Carl Nash. The trapeze student was standing by a lion's cage, and he had a big smile on his face.

"Justine," he drawled, opening his arms. "I've been waiting for you."

Justine ran up to him, handed him the ball, and the two embraced. Nash lifted his head to say something to Justine. Then he spotted Frank and Joe, and his smile faded. Even in their clown disguises, Nash must have known who they were.

"Hey, you guys," Nash said nervously. "Great getup." He forced a smile and pushed Justine away. Joe noticed that Nash glanced hastily off to the side. Unless he was wrong, the trapeze student was looking for an escape route.

"Nice to see you, too, Carl," Frank said. "We

found Justine waiting in the hall by clown alley. She said you two were meeting up."

"Oh?" Nash gave Justine a questioning look.

"These guys asked me all kinds of questions about the man who gave me that ball," Justine told Nash. "I said if they wanted answers, they should ask you. I told them I was just doing you a favor."

The glare that Nash gave Justine was unmistakable. Joe could tell that he was trying to control his anger. Then his face relaxed and he gave Justine a smile.

"Thanks, hon," Nash said. "I know I can always count on you." He leaned against the lion's cage and continued to smile at Justine. The lion inside the cage stood up and let out a small roar. Nash glanced at the lion and casually backed away from the cage.

Then, with a lightning movement, Nash dashed past Frank and Joe, in the direction of the doorway. Frank reacted swiftly, sticking out his leg to trip Nash. The trapeze student went flying to the ground in front of the lion's cage. This time, the lion let out an even louder roar. As Nash fell, the ball flew out of his hands into the air.

Joe watched in horror as the juggler's ball flew through the bars and landed right in the lion's cage.

13 Into the Lion's Den

While Joe's eyes were still on the ball that was lying inside the lion's cage, Nash jumped up and delivered a sharp blow to his jaw.

Joe sank to his knees, dizzy from the punch. The polka dots on his costume swam in front of his eyes. He held his head for a moment, and heard Frank call out his name.

"Get up, Joe!" Frank cried. "Help me out."

Joe opened his eyes to see Frank wrestling with Nash on the sawdust-covered floor. Nash was on top and had Frank pinned. The circus performance had started, and there was no one else in the area to stop the fight.

Joe raced over to Frank and pulled Nash off his

brother. Then he drew back his fist and hit Nash hard in the stomach. Nash bent over, holding his middle, then slowly sank to the floor beside the lion's cage.

Justine rushed over and fell on her knees in front of him. Nash used her support to stand up. The trapeze student stood rubbing his chin. "You guys are good," he said, nodding thoughtfully at Frank and Joe. "Too good, in fact."

With that, Nash lashed out at Joe, punching him in the face. As Joe went down, Nash karate-kicked Frank in the stomach, and Frank fell in a heap next to Joe.

Joe tried to stand up, but Nash's second punch had made his ears ring. His wig had gotten knocked off and was lying on the ground next to him. Finally, Joe's head stopped throbbing, and he was able to get to his feet.

Frank got to his feet slowly. His costume was covered with sawdust, his wig was sideways on his head, and he was clutching his stomach. Justine hurried over to him and asked him if he was okay. Frank nodded, his pain making it difficult to speak.

"Did you see which way he went?" Joe asked Justine. Justine shook her head silently and swallowed a few times.

"He's gone by now," Frank said, looking toward the doorway. "And if I'm right, he's not coming back either," he added in disgust.

119

Joe nodded. "He's probably running off right now with his buddy, Ralph Rosen."

"I'm telling you, you've got it all wrong," Justine insisted. "I know Carl Nash, and he's no criminal."

"So why'd he take us out like that?" Joe asked. "Innocent people don't just go around punching out other guys. Come on, Justine. Carl Nash is involved in something dishonest and dangerous. Why don't you tell us what it is?"

Frank shot his brother a warning look, as if to remind him to go easy on the girl. Justine gave Joe a steely look. "I've told you everything I know. I'm going to find an animal trainer to get that ball out of there," she said, pointing to the lion's cage, where the lion had started sniffing at the ball that had landed there. "Then you'll see that there's nothing suspicious going on."

"You're saying that's just an ordinary juggler's ball Rosen wanted your friend Carl to have?" Joe asked.

Justine glared at Joe and turned to speak to Frank. "I'll be back." With that, she strode out of the room.

Frank turned to his brother and made a face. "You sure do have a way with women," he said sarcastically. "Nice work, Joe."

Joe kicked at the sawdust on the ground with his foot. Frank was right. He had been a little harsh with Justine, but only because he was getting frustrated by all the dead ends. "She's got to know something," Joe insisted. "Nash is a close buddy of hers. He sent her to get the ball from Rosen, then tried to take off when we showed up."

"But Justine stayed behind after Nash finally left," Frank reminded his brother. "She didn't take off with him."

Joe realized Frank had a point. "You really think she doesn't know anything?"

"I don't know," Frank said. He rubbed his sore stomach. "She doesn't seem to."

"But her initials are on the list," Joe insisted.

"So are Georgianne Unger's," Frank said.

Joe looked inside the lion's cage. The lion had started nibbling at the ball. "All this is speculation until we find out if there's another message in that ball," Joe said. "And if there is, we've got to get it before that big cat does."

The lion yawned and shook his mane. Then he put his paws on the ball and started biting at it in earnest. Frank grabbed a whip that was hanging on a hook attached to the cage. Then he stepped near to the cage.

"What are you going to do?" Joe asked.

"We've got to get the ball away from him," Frank told his brother, holding on tightly to the whip. The lion seemed to be keeping an eye on them while he pawed away at the ball.

121

"If there's a message inside the ball," Joe said, "that lion's going to get at it. Hurry."

"I am hurrying," Frank insisted as he uncoiled the whip.

"But be careful, too," Joe warned.

Frank nodded. He stepped back a few paces and drew back the whip, keeping his eyes on a spot about a foot in front of the lion. Then he snapped the whip. It flew through the bars and hit the floor of the cage with a loud *crack.* The lion opened his jaws wide and let out a huge roar.

"Hey!" Joe shouted, jumping back.

"Keep cool," Frank said, quietly. He snapped the whip at the spot in front of the lion again. This time the lion jumped up and backed away, leaving the ball behind.

"Hurry!" Joe yelled. "Get the ball."

Frank quickly snapped the whip at the ball, sending it flying into the far corner of the cage. The lion roared again, louder this time, and began to paw at the whip.

"Grab the ball!" Frank told Joe. "I'll keep him back!"

Joe darted to the side of the cage and swiftly reached his hand inside. He had almost managed to grab the ball when he heard a voice call out. "Hey, you! Get your hands out of there!"

Joe turned to see Justine standing in the doorway with a man by her side. The man rushed over, pulled Joe away from the cage, and held him by the shoulders.

"What do you . . . clowns . . . think you're doing?" he demanded.

Joe was about to explain when Frank stepped up. "That's our ball in there," he said. "We were trying to get it out."

"Real smart," the man said, letting go of Joe. "You guys could have been killed." With that, he grabbed the whip out of Frank's hand, unlocked the cage, and stepped inside. In a few trained movements, the man had the lion sitting back on his hind legs, his paws in the air. "Stay, Brutus," the man told the lion sharply. He then walked over to the corner of the cage and picked up the ball. He tossed it through the bars of the cage, and Joe caught it neatly between his hands.

"Thanks!" Joe yelled out.

"Next time," the man warned, "don't mess with these animals. They may be trained, but that doesn't stop them from attacking." He passed the lion a tidbit from his pocket, backed out of the cage, and locked it up.

Frank took the ball from Joe and wiped it clean. He looked it over carefully. "Is there anything inside?" Joe asked his brother.

"Nope," Frank said. He tried twisting the ball, but Joe could see it wouldn't budge.

"Now are you satisfied?" Justine asked, her

arms crossed in front of her. "If you're through with the ball, I'd like to give it back to Carl."

"Not so fast," Joe told her. He took the ball back from Frank and examined it himself. His brother was right—there was no way of opening it up, which meant there had to be something else important about it. He looked at the gems carefully. Like the ones on the other ball, these looked like rhinestones, about an inch in size each.

"Is there a knife around?" he asked the animal trainer. The man gave Joe a quizzical look but pulled a pocketknife from his pants pocket and gave it to Joe.

Joe opened the knife and scratched away at one of the gems. It broke into a few pieces and fell to the ground.

"Rhinestones?" Frank asked, realizing what his brother was up to.

"Or glass," Joe replied. "Let's try another." One by one, Joe scratched at the gems, and one by one, all of them broke into pieces.

"Give it up, Joe," Frank suggested. "This is another dead end."

But Joe wasn't about to give in so easily. He knew there had to be a reason why Rosen and Nash had acted so suspiciously, and this ball held the clue. He went at the last gem. He scratched its surface, expecting it to fall apart, too. But it didn't. Instead, the gem shone out even more brilliantly. Joe caught his breath, realizing what they'd found.

"Not a scratch!" he announced, his voice rising in excitement.

Frank took one look at the gem and let out a long whistle. "You don't mean . . . ?"

Joe nodded. "Unless I'm wrong, we've got our hands on a real diamond!"

14 Cracking the Code

Justine gasped and looked nervously at Frank and Joe. Frank braced himself, ready to stop her from running off. If she was involved, he was sure she'd try to get away.

But the trapeze student just stood there, staring at the ball. "No," she said softly, her eyes filling with tears. "Not Carl."

"Not Carl?" Joe repeated. "Just what do you know about this, Justine?" he demanded, holding up the ball.

Justine hid her face in her hands. Frank went over to her and put his hand on her arm. "It's okay," he told her. "Why don't you calm down, and then you can tell us what you know." He took the ball from Joe. "Did you know Rosen

126

was passing diamonds to Nash?" Frank asked quietly.

"I knew the ball was important," Justine said, holding back her tears. "Carl told me to meet that guy at exactly eleven o'clock, but he also told me that if anything happened, I should hold on to the ball no matter what and pretend I didn't know anything. Which I don't, really."

Joe tapped his foot impatiently. "You knew more than you were letting on before," he insisted.

"That's enough, Joe," Frank said firmly. He turned to Justine and asked, "Why couldn't Carl meet Rosen himself?"

Justine wiped a tear from her eye. "He said it was too dangerous, with you guys prowling around. He said Rosen would understand why he needed an intermediary."

"So Carl picked you," Frank concluded, feeling sorry for the young woman. "Weren't you worried it would be dangerous for you?" he asked.

"I love Carl," Justine confessed. "I'd do anything for him."

"But now you see what kind of person he is," Joe said. "It looks like he's messed up with the theft of a diamond, at the very least," he said.

Frank followed through on Joe's reasoning. "Nash and Rosen are accomplices in something illegal. They're doing their best to hide it by passing juggler's balls and coded messages back and forth. And now that we know this ball has a diamond in it, I'm beginning to wonder if we're looking at a smuggling ring or the theft of one diamond."

"What did you mean just now about coded messages?" Justine asked, her eyes wide.

Joe quickly explained about the code and told Justine that her initials were in it, too. "Did Carl tell you to plan to meet Rosen again on January third?" he asked, referring to the date that corresponded to Justine's initials on the code.

Justine shook her head. "No. I'm going back to Florida after the circus is finished in Bayport. My family is there, and I want to spend Christmas and New Year's with them. Nash is going home, too."

"Rats," Frank said, realizing their theory was shot again. Nash could be using Justine to pick up another of Rosen's drops, but only if both Rosen and Justine were on tour together. "Did Nash ever ask you to continue with the tour in January?" he pressed, trying to fit the facts into the theory.

"No," Justine said again. "Look, I don't know what Carl is involved in, but I'm sure there's got to be an explanation," she said, trying to sound convincing. But one look at the ball in Frank's hands made her cut the speech short. "I've got to go," Justine said abruptly. "I have to get ready for our performances this afternoon. Circus U. students are putting on a show for the Montero, and I need to get ready."

Frank watched the trapeze student leave and then turned to his brother. "This is even more serious than we thought," he said, rubbing his finger over the diamond. "Jewel thieves as well as sabotage."

"And we still don't even know why the sabotage is taking place or how it's connected to the diamond," Joe added, as he began to take off his clown suit.

Frank started to remove his costume, too. "Why would Rosen have dropped the message two days ago, and then the diamond today?" he asked, as he slipped off the oversize clown shoes. "And how did Nash know to meet Rosen, or send Justine, when the first message never got to him?"

"Ah, that's much better," Joe said, flexing his arms. "I'm really glad to be out of that costume."

"So, how did Nash know to meet Rosen?" Frank repeated.

Joe thought for a moment. "Maybe Nash had another meeting with Rosen yesterday. Maybe that's when they arranged this meeting."

"That could be why we saw Rosen around here yesterday," Frank agreed. "But here's another

129

question: Why would Rosen be giving Nash instructions about other drops in the first place—assuming that's what the message means?"

"Especially since, as Justine says, she and Nash aren't continuing with the tour," Joe put in. "Nash couldn't help Rosen out then."

"True," Frank said. Then something occurred to him. "Hey," he said, snapping his fingers. "What if Nash is only one part of this whole thing?"

"Huh?" Joe asked, the confusion evident on his face. "You're not making sense. Who else would be involved?"

"Nash was meant to get the message instead of Chet, right?" Frank said, testing his theory. "But who sent Nash to work the table that night?"

"The same person who sent Chet," Joe replied. "Bo Costello."

"Right!" Frank exclaimed. He pocketed the ball and grabbed Joe's arm. "I think we've found the missing link."

Moments later, Frank and Joe were standing outside Bo Costello's office. The admissions director wasn't in, and the door was locked tight.

"This is our first real break," Joe said, trying the knob.

"We'd better make this search a quick one," Frank said. "We don't know when Costello will be back." He found a large safety pin lying on the floor. He picked it up and bent it straight. "This will do just fine." Frank stuck the pin in the lock and twisted it back and forth. In a few seconds he heard the lock click open. "Be careful," he warned. "Keep your ears and eyes open. We don't want to get caught here."

Joe nodded and followed his brother inside Costello's office. He locked the door shut behind them and braced a chair against it, figuring that the barrier would buy them some time if Costello showed up. "What are we looking for, anyway?"

"Some kind of proof that Costello knows Rosen better than he says he does," Frank told him. "If Nash had been working alone with Costello, Rosen wouldn't have needed to pass him instructions or information in that message. He would have dropped the ball with the diamond on it and that would have been that."

Frank remembered the conversation they'd overheard the day before between Costello and one of his former students. The director of admissions had told the person on the other end of the line to "be careful." He reminded Joe about what they had heard. "Maybe he was talking to Rosen."

Joe wandered over to the bulletin board on Costello's wall. "That's a good guess. Hey," Joe added, "check this out." He stood by the bulletin board and pointed at one of the sheets Costello had tacked onto it.

Frank went over to the bulletin board and

looked at the photographs. He was hoping there would be one of Costello together with Rosen, something that showed they were partners in crime. It was stretching it, he knew, but there had to be some kind of proof to his theory somewhere in Costello's office.

"Look at these marks. Right here, next to these dates," Joe said. "I mean, why these dates in particular? What's so important about them?"

Frank saw a small smile on Joe's face as he leaned over to look where his brother was pointing. "December twentieth. January third. February fourteenth. This is the Montero schedule," Joe said. "Bo Costello's made little marks next to all three of these dates. He's even got initials next to them—his own little code, I guess."

Frank copied the dates down once again, along with the list of towns where the Montero was going to be on those dates. "Bayport we know," he said. "On January third, the Montero's going to be in Indianapolis, Indiana."

"And on the fourteenth of February, it'll stop in Fort Worth, Texas," Joe read from the list. "But the initials next to the dates aren't the same ones we've got on our list," he added, frustrated.

Frank sat down at Costello's desk and started playing with the numbers and the towns. He abbreviated the cities and came up with BP,

IN and FW. "Look," he said, showing the list to Joe. "What if we make this into a code all its own."

Joe scratched his head and looked over Frank's shoulder. "You mean, put the dates with the abbreviations you've got there?"

"Exactly," Frank said. "And next to that, we'll put the initials from Rosen's original list."

"Okay," Joe said. "For twelve-twenty, we've got BP—that's short for Bayport—and CN from Rosen's list."

"And for one-oh-three, there's IN—Indianap-olis—and JL," Frank went on. "That leaves two-fourteen, FW and GU."

"Hey," Joe said slowly. "I think I see some-thing."

"You do?" Frank asked.

Joe pointed at the letters. "Look. If you go down the alphabet one letter from *B*, you get *C*. And then if you go back up through the alphabet two letters from *P*, you get *N*."

Frank looked at the rest of the list and realized Joe was right. "Check it out!" he cried. "Take IN. Add a letter to the *I* and you get *J*. Subtract two letters from the *N* and you get *L*. JL becomes IN."

"And we thought Justine was the next victim of sabotage, or the next person to get passed one of Rosen's balls," Joe said. "What the list really means is that the next drop is going to take place in Indianapolis. The people's initials were just used to make the code."

"And GU—which we thought meant Georgianne Unger," Frank concluded, "really means Fort Worth."

"Rosen really was passing information to Costello," Joe said, shaking his head in wonder. "And the list doesn't seem to have a thing to do with the sabotage."

"Or does it?" Frank wondered aloud. He tapped the desk firmly with his fist. "Bo Costello's got a lot of explaining to do. Come on."

"Where are we going?" Joe asked.

"We're going to find him and ask him point-blank if he's working a smuggling ring with Ralph Rosen," Frank said with determination.

Joe glanced at the door and saw the chair he'd braced against it start to move. The doorknob was turning. "Uh, Frank," he said, "I don't think that's going to be necessary."

"What?" Frank shot Joe a quizzical look. "Why not?"

"Because my guess is he's on his way in here," Joe said in a harsh whisper.

Frank looked at the door and saw the knob turn. His eyes moved around the room for an escape, but there was no window and nowhere to hide.

"What are we going to do?" he asked Joe, his eyes fixed on the door.

"There's nothing we can do," Joe shot back.

With that, the door burst open. Standing there, with Carl Nash by his side, was Bo Costello. And he did not look at all happy to see the Hardys.

15 Fireworks!

"Well, well," Costello said, smiling broadly at the Hardys. "Looks like we got our hands on a couple of clowns. Without the costumes, but still in full makeup."

Nash gave the two of them a wicked smile. "Maybe they were just looking for an application," he said. "Or someone to help them with that makeup."

"Actually, we were looking for a couple of crooks," Joe shot back. "And it looks like we found them."

Frank grabbed onto his brother's arm. "Keep your head," he warned under his breath.

Costello raised his eyebrows. "Crooks?" he said in a surprised tone. "We're not crooks. Just good businessmen." Nash began to laugh, but Costello cut him off. "That's enough," he said. "The circus isn't all fun and games, you know. But I guess you two have already discovered that," he added, nodding at Frank and Joe.

"We know about your diamond theft," Joe fired. "You're not going to get away with it."

"But I already have," Costello said softly. "And, once the two of you are out of the way, I will continue to."

"Continue to?" Joe said. "So you *are* smuggling diamonds."

Costello smiled. "Clever of you to have figured that out."

Frank stood his ground, waiting for the moment to make his move. If they planned it right, between them, he and Joe could take on Nash and Costello. It was just a matter of timing.

Costello stepped into his office and closed the door behind him. "Now, what are we going to do with these two?" he asked Nash.

Nash showed his teeth in a gruesome smile. "I say we throw them to the lions."

"Oh, please," Costello said in a calm voice. "Be serious."

"Once the word gets out about what you've been up to, your scheme is dead," Frank told the director of admissions.

Costello shook his head sadly. "You're not telling me anything I don't already know. That's why we have to do something with you two, before you manage to tell anyone else." He stepped over to his desk and pulled a box of fireworks out from underneath it. He took a stick of fireworks out of the box and unwound the fuse.

"What are you going to do?" Joe asked.

"There's going to be a little accident here," Costello explained, holding up the stick. "I suppose I shouldn't keep something as dangerous as this here, but fireworks are my specialty."

"Then it was you who caused that uncontrolled explosion," Frank said, remembering what Paul Turner had told them about the fireworks accident at Circus U.

Costello tapped his head with the fireworks stick. "You boys are so smart. Nash, there's a lighter in my bag next to the two boys. Get it." he ordered.

Nash came over to Frank and Joe, his head down, looking for the bag. Frank got ready to make his move, keeping his eyes on Nash. Nash just had to step a little closer, and then—

But before he could make his move, Joe lunged at Nash.

In a flash, Bo Costello reached across the desk and grabbed Joe's arms. Joe felt himself fall backward onto the desk. He struggled to free himself from Costello's grip.

Frank started for Costello. Then he felt a sharp pain in his left side, and he collapsed onto the floor.

"Good work, Carl," Costello bellowed.

Then Frank heard Costello let out a grunt. Frank raised his head to see that Joe had broken free and had punched Costello in the stomach.

Frank got to his feet in time to see Nash coming toward him. Frank did a double take and turned to face Nash. The trapeze artist came flying at him, his feet outstretched in a karate move.

Frank braced himself for the blow. Nash came at him feetfirst. Frank began to duck, but Nash reacted swiftly. Frank felt Nash's feet make contact with his stomach. The blow sent him flying backward onto Costello's desk to land on his back. Getting to his feet, Frank saw out of the corner of his eye that Joe was still wrestling with Costello.

Nash came in on Frank to finish the job. Frank shot his right hand out to ward Nash off, but Nash sneered, drew his arm up to protect himself, and socked Frank in the chin.

Frank fell off the desk in a heap. He heard Joe grunt several times, then saw his brother fall to the floor next to him.

"They've got us," Joe said with a groan. "We're goners."

"No way," Frank mumbled back. He felt himself getting dizzy from the force of Nash's blow. He had to stay awake. He just had to.

Frank closed his eyes for a second and felt someone tying his hands together. "Not too tight," Costello warned. "We want them to be able to get free, so there's no sign that we tied them. Too bad it won't be in time for them to escape."

Nash grunted and continued to tie Frank's hands together. Frank was just about to lash out with his legs when he felt Nash grasp them hard and tie them together, too. One look at Joe out of the corner of his eye told Frank his brother was in the same mess.

At their heads, Frank saw Costello drop a pile of fireworks onto the desk, along with the fireworks stick he had been holding. The fuse was long, but not long enough to give the Hardys much time. With one last, wicked grin, Costello reached out with a flourish and held a lighter to the fuse.

"Goodbye, kids," Costello called out as he flicked off the lights. "It's been nice knowing you."

With that, Costello shut the door. Frank heard it lock behind him. In the silence that followed, he heard the sound of the fuse burning.

"Quick, Joe!" he cried out, wriggling his hands until he could feel the knot Nash had used to tie them together. He worked at the knot and managed to untie it. He quickly untied his legs.

"We've got to get out of here. This place is going to blow!"

Joe pulled himself to a sitting position and waited impatiently for Frank to untie his hands. While he freed his legs, Frank raced over to the fireworks.

Costello had lashed together more than twenty fireworks. The one that was burning now would set off a reaction that would cause a huge explosion—one that might not only kill them, but was sure to cause serious damage. There was no time to waste!

Frank raced to the door. He tried the knob and found it was locked from the outside. Joe came rushing over to him and tried it, too, but it was no use. They were locked in.

"Get back!" Joe cried. He darted to the back of the room and came rushing toward the door, his shoulder lowered.

Frank watched as his brother propelled himself into the door, landing square against it. The force bashed the door off its hinges.

"Good work!" Frank cried. He kicked the door off its hinges and raced outside. "Come on, quick. We've got to get out of here."

Joe dashed into the hallway. At that moment, the fireworks blew, and Costello's office exploded in a riot of red, white, and blue lights.

"Wow!" Joe said, staring at the display. "That was too close."

"You said it," Frank said. At that moment, Paul

Turner came running down the hall. Chet was at his side.

"What happened?" the dean asked. He took one look at Costello's office and turned to Frank and Joe.

"There's no time to explain!" Frank yelled. "We've got to catch Costello and Nash."

"Costello?" Chet asked, shaking his head in confusion. "Nash? Why?"

"Forget it," Joe said. "Look!"

Joe was pointing down the long hallway. Costello's back was just visible as the director of admissions turned the corner toward the stairwell. "There they are!" Joe yelled.

With that, Joe took off at a run after them. Frank followed closely behind. Their chase led them up the stairs, past the performers in the backstage area, and into the arena. The seats were beginning to fill up with people. The audience stared at the Hardys as they chased Costello and Nash across the ring.

"What are they doing?" Frank asked, watching as Costello and Nash separated and climbed the ladders that led to the trapeze swings.

"I don't know, but I'm going after them," Joe cried. He raced to the ladder on one side of the ring. "Take the other one," he cried to Frank.

Frank didn't take time to think about what he was about to do. He rushed to the ladder and started climbing it, trying not to think about the fact that he was climbing thirty feet off the ground. When he remembered the safety net, he felt better.

Nash was a few feet ahead of him on the ladder. Frank reached out to grab the man's ankle, but Nash yanked his leg free and kept climbing.

Frank took a moment to look for Joe. His brother was following Costello up the other ladder, but Costello had a good lead. The director of admissions was nearly to the top. Frank saw another, smaller ladder extending up from the platform onto a catwalk that held the lights and ran around the ceiling of the arena.

"Stop him!" Frank cried to Joe. "He's going to get away!"

16 High-Wire High Jinks

Joe heard his brother's warning and craned his neck up the ladder. He saw Costello move along the platform toward the smaller ladder that led to the catwalk.

Joe gripped the ladder and took the rungs three at a time. In a flash, he was up at the top and had grabbed onto Costello's leg. The man tried to pull it free, but Joe kept his hold tight.

"I give up!" Costello cried. "You've got me. I give up."

Joe came down the small ladder onto the platform. "Easy does it," he warned. "Or we're both going to fall."

"Don't worry," Costello said, "I'm ready to come down."

Joe felt a wave of relief as he started down the ladder. He looked up, expecting to see Costello following him. But instead he saw Costello smiling down at him. "That was a great escape," he said. "You kids are tougher than I thought."

Joe kept his eyes on Costello. He wasn't going to let himself be tricked again. "You're coming down with me," Joe warned. "Let's go. And no funny business."

Costello laughed. "Of course not."

Joe waited for the director of admissions to start down the ladder. Without warning, though, Costello turned and grabbed a trapeze swing and unhooked it from the platform. Before Joe could react, the man had stepped off the platform and was swept away on the trapeze.

Joe climbed back up to the platform and surveyed the situation. Costello was swinging back and forth between the trapeze platforms. Across the way on the other ladder, Joe could see Frank struggling with Carl Nash, trying to prevent the man from escaping onto the catwalk on that side. His brother couldn't help Joe out now. There was only one choice—take the other trapeze swing and go!

Joe grabbed the swing from where it was hooked up next to him, took a deep breath, tried not to look down, and swung off the platform.

Before Joe knew it, he was flying through the

air in a long, breathtaking arch. The ground swelled away from him, up and back, up and back. He kept his grip firm on the trapeze swing and timed the motion. Next to him, Costello was still swinging back and forth, timing his swings so that they would miss Joe.

Joe lashed out with his legs, trying to catch Costello as he swung by, but the move failed. Instead of stopping Costello, Joe just made his trapeze swing wildly. He almost lost control of the trapeze, but he straightened out his legs at the last minute and regained his balance.

But Costello used that time to let himself land back on the same platform from which he'd jumped. There wasn't any time to waste. Joe had to get back there, too. There was just one problem: Joe still had his back to the platform. He was going to have to turn around!

Trying to remember a move he'd seen the night before, Joe held his breath and said to himself, "Here goes nothing." With that, he let go of the swing with one hand.

Joe heard the unmistakable sound of the crowd below drawing in a long breath. For a split-second he was airborne, then he swiftly twisted himself around and caught the trapeze swing with the other hand. He did it!

Without wasting another second, Joe landed squarely on the trapeze platform. Bo Costello was waiting for him. As soon as Joe felt the platform under his feet, he also felt Costello's fist meet his jaw.

The blow made Joe lose his balance, but at the last second, he caught the ladder with his right hand. In the same movement, Joe lashed out with his left leg, catching Costello right in the stomach.

The director of admissions let out a low groan. Joe looked on in disbelief as Costello stumbled on the platform, lost his balance, and finally fell thirty feet down into the safety net.

"One down, one to go," Joe muttered under his breath.

Across the way, on the other platform, Frank was fighting Carl Nash. The two were trading punches, and Frank seemed to be subduing the trapeze student. But then Joe saw Nash give Frank a punch in the stomach that made him fall to his knees.

"Here we go again," Joe said, grabbing onto the trapeze swing. He took off and felt himself flying through the air yet again. "I'm getting pretty good at this," Joe said to himself. He heard the roar of the crowd in the bleachers below him as he went sailing through the air.

A second later, Joe had landed square on the platform across the way. Over his head, he saw Frank climbing up the small ladder after Nash. "Keep cool," Joe shouted to his brother. "I'm coming up."

But soon Joe realized Frank didn't need his help. Just as he reached the ladder, Joe saw Carl Nash come flying down in front of his eyes—and right into the safety net next to his partner in crime, Bo Costello. The two men were caught at last.

It was early evening, and Frank and Joe were in Dean Turner's office. They had just finished filling in the dean, Georgianne, and Justine on what Costello had been up to.

"I simply cannot believe that a man like Bo Costello, someone with his history of devotion and commitment to the circus, would stoop so low," Dean Turner said, shaking his head sadly. "After such a brilliant career."

"Believe it, Paul," Georgianne Unger said, "and be glad these guys figured it out."

"What's really sad is that Costello was using Nash, a really promising circus performer, to further his scheme," Joe said.

Justine sighed deeply and shook her head. "I can't believe I trusted him," was all she could say.

"I just hope the police manage to find Ralph Rosen," Chet offered. "I'd hate to see that guy get away."

Frank rubbed his eyes. "They'll find him," he said with assurance. "He can't get too far in a Montero Brothers Circus van. And they'll find the other circus performers who were helping Costello out with his scheme, too. All the evidence is right there in Costello's office."

"How'd he manage to do it?" Turner said, confused.

"Costello made contacts with jewel thieves all across the country. It wasn't hard to convince them that the circus would make a great cover for smuggling—all those places to hide gems, easy contact, plus his connection to former students in circuses all over the country."

"And the students went along with it?" Georgianne asked.

"Costello convinced them that the money involved was a lot better than what they'd make just working for the circus," Frank said. "And don't forget, he picked his people very carefully."

"People like Carl Nash," Chet said sadly.

"But why did he need to use his former students?" Turner asked.

"It gave him a larger circle of smugglers to work with," Joe explained. "Rosen was only one of his operatives."

"Why didn't Costello make contact with Rosen himself this time?" Justine asked. "Why did he have to use Carl?"

"My guess is that Costello was using this time to train Nash, who was graduating this year," Frank said. "He wanted to make sure Nash could do it."

"And Nash helped Costello with the sabotage, too," Joe said. "The gunpowder in the cannon was his doing. And sawing through the stilts, too."

"And Nash was the guy who broke into my brother's room to steal Rosen's ball," Frank said. "It looks as if he also helped Costello sabotage the clown makeup and let the tiger loose from his cage."

"What about that accident on the trapeze?" Justine asked.

"That was a smoke screen so Joe and I wouldn't suspect Carl," Frank said. "Costello planned it. He knew Nash wouldn't really get hurt."

"I can't believe Bo did all this just so he could make me look incompetent," Turner said, his voice rising in anger.

"He wanted you out of the way," Joe added. "He was sure that the so-called accidents would make the trustees fire you and put him in your place as dean."

"Then he'd have even more freedom to travel and train his people," Frank went on. "He had it all worked out."

"What about the message?" Turner wanted to know. "Was that really instructions to Costello about the next drops that were going to take place?"

Joe ran his hands through his hair. "It looks like it. Rosen was the middleman between

Costello and his contacts. Rosen would get the information from a thief about when and where a jewel would be ready to be smuggled. Then Rosen would pass that information to Costello, who would set up one of his former students to pick up the gem. Then the student turned the gem over to Costello, who would fence it."

"The process ensured that no one had the gems for too long," Frank said. "So that no one person could be pinpointed as the smuggler."

"When Rosen disappeared two nights ago," Joe added, "he'd gone to get the diamond that he was planning to smuggle to Nash."

"Costello admitted that he handled everything out of Circus U.," Frank said. "But he never had to have contact with the thieves himself. That way, he was protected in case something went wrong. He thought that all those messages would prevent him from being connected too closely to the smuggling ring."

"Pretty clever," Chet said softly.

"Well, I'm just glad the whole thing is over." Dean Turner took his glasses off and wiped them gently with his handkerchief. "Now we can all look forward to the rest of the Montero Brothers Circus tour. And Circus U. can return to its normal business—training top-notch circus performers, not crooks and thieves."

Georgianne gave Turner a slow smile. "With me as director of admissions, you can be sure I'll

151

accept only the most honest, dedicated students."

"Not like Bo Costello," Chet countered.

"Right," Georgianne said.

"People like Chet Morton, for example?" Joe asked, raising an eyebrow.

"Possibly," she said with a small smile. "We'll have to wait and see how the rest of his classes go *and* his performance Friday night."

Justine laughed out loud. "I'm sure it will go just fine, now that he can really get down to business."

"Now that Frank and Joe Hardy have solved the crime," Turner said, putting his glasses back on, "I can't thank you boys enough."

Joe smiled, and Frank reached out to shake the dean's hand. "You're welcome," he said.

"I have to thank you guys, too," Chet said with a grin. "Now I can finally get down to some serious clowning!"